MARVEL

MARVEL ACTION

AVENGERS

THE RUBY EGRESS

Marvel Publishing:

Jeff Youngquist: VP Production & Special Projects
Caitlin O'Connell: Assistant Editor, Special Projects
Sven Larsen: Director, Licensed Publishing
David Gabriel: SVP Print, Sales & Marketing
C.B. Cebulski: Editor In Chief
Joe Quesada: Chief Creative Officer
Dan Buckley: President, Marvel Entertainment
Alan Fine: Executive Producer

IDW Publishing:

IDW

Chris Ryall, President and Publisher/CCO
John Barber, Editor-In-Chief
Cara Morrison, Chief Financial Officer

Collection Edits
JUSTIN EISINGER
and **ALONZO SIMON**

Matt Ruzicka, Chief Accounting Officer
David Hedgecock, Associate Publisher
Jerry Bennington, VP of New Product Development

Collection Design
CHRISTA MIESNER

Lorelei Bunjes, VP of Digital Services
Justin Eisinger, Editorial Director, Graphic Novels & Collections
Eric Moss, Senior Director, Licensing and Business Development

Cover Art by
JON SOMMARIVA

Ted Adams and Robbie Robbins, Founders of IDW

ISBN: 978-1-68405-522-7   22 21 20 19   1 2 3 4

Special thanks: **Tom Brevoort**

Originally published as MARVEL ACTION: AVENGERS issues #4-6

For international rights, contact licensing@idwpublishing.com

MARVEL

MARVEL ACTION

AVENGERS

THE RUBY EGRESS

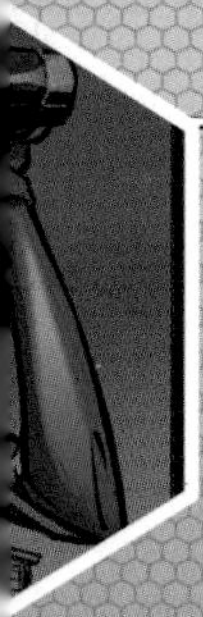

WRITTEN BY MATTHEW K. MANNING

ART BY JON SOMMARIVA

ADDITIONAL INKS BY SEAN PARSONS AND JIMMY REYES

COLORS BY PROTOBUNKER

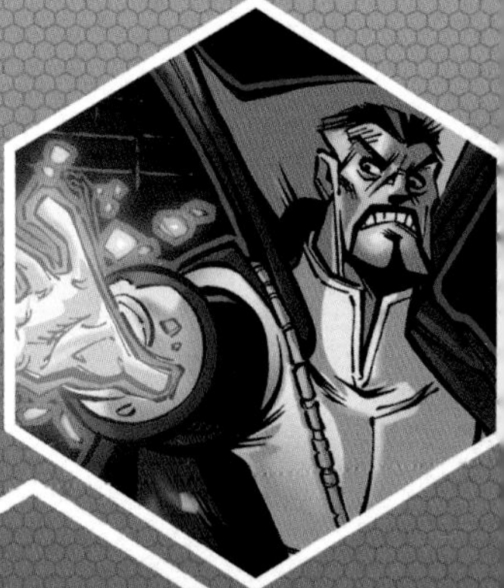

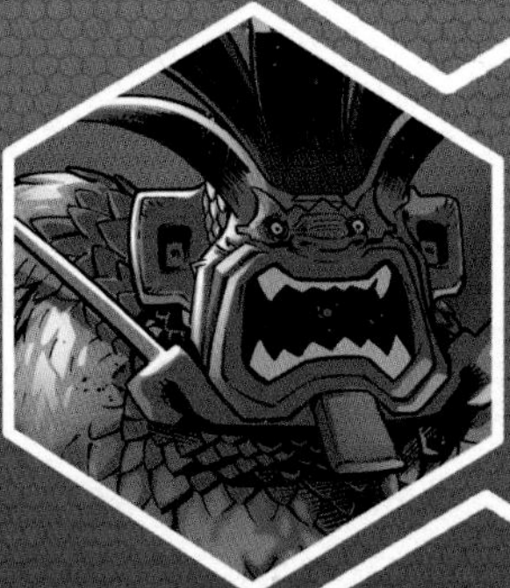

LETTERS BY CHRISTA MIESNER

ASSISTANT EDITS BY MEGAN BROWN

EDITED BY BOBBY CURNOW

EDITOR IN CHIEF JOHN BARBER

AVENGERS CREATED BY
STAN LEE & JACK KIRBY

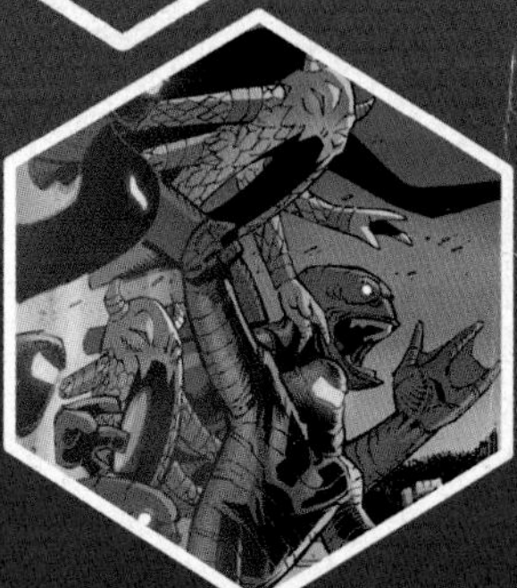

ART BY: JON SOMMARIVA

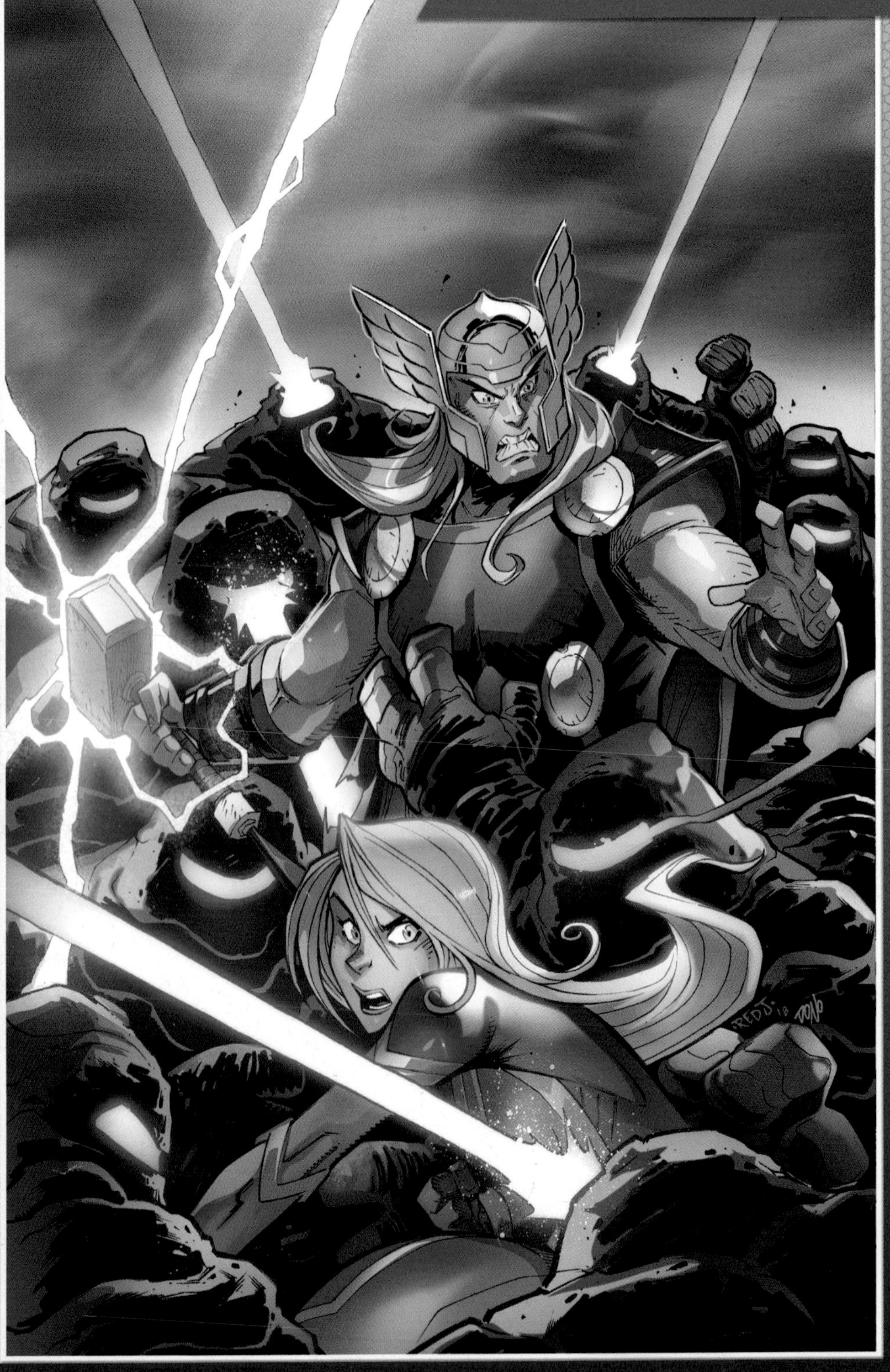

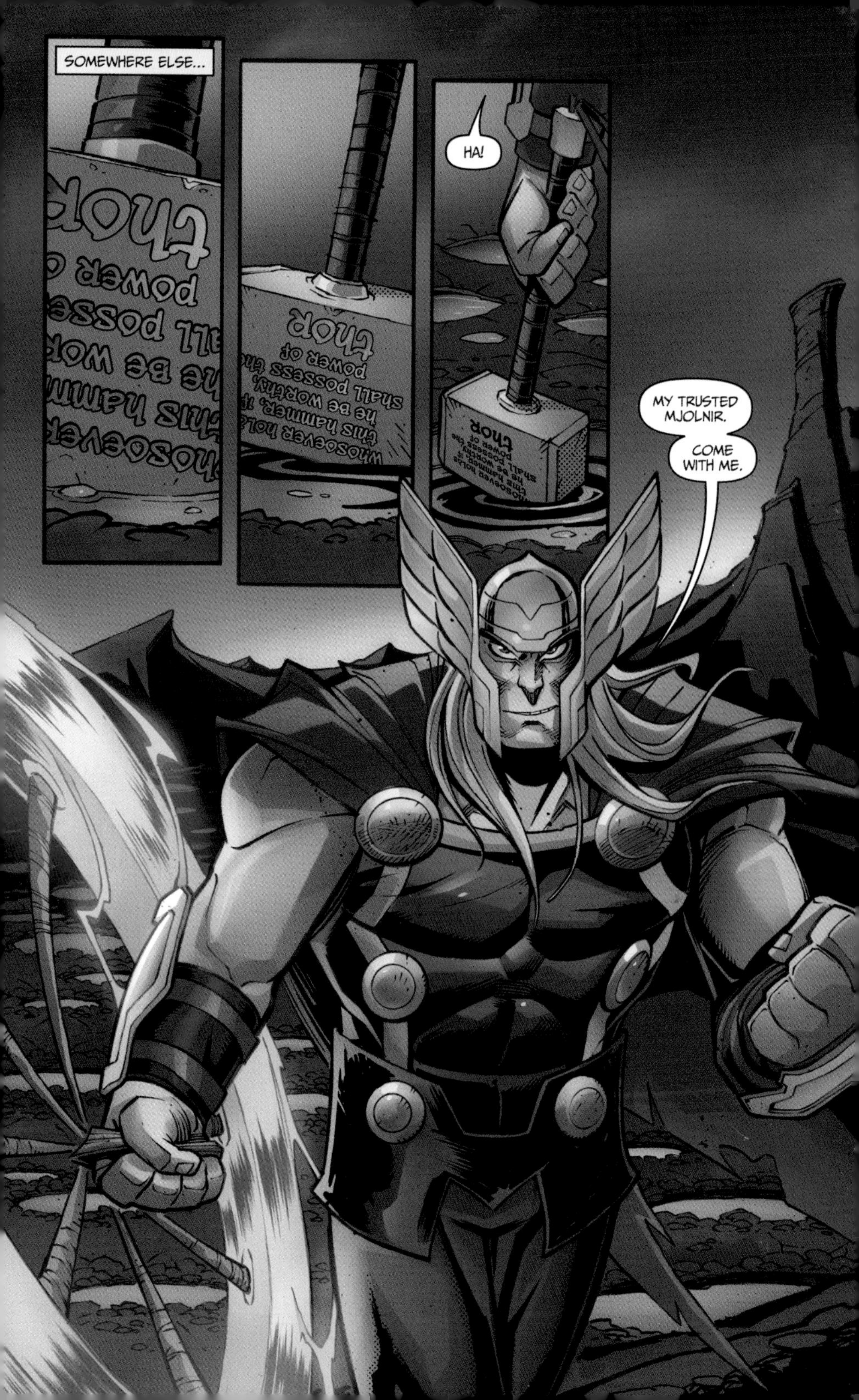
SOMEWHERE ELSE...
HA!
MY TRUSTED MJOLNIR.
COME WITH ME.

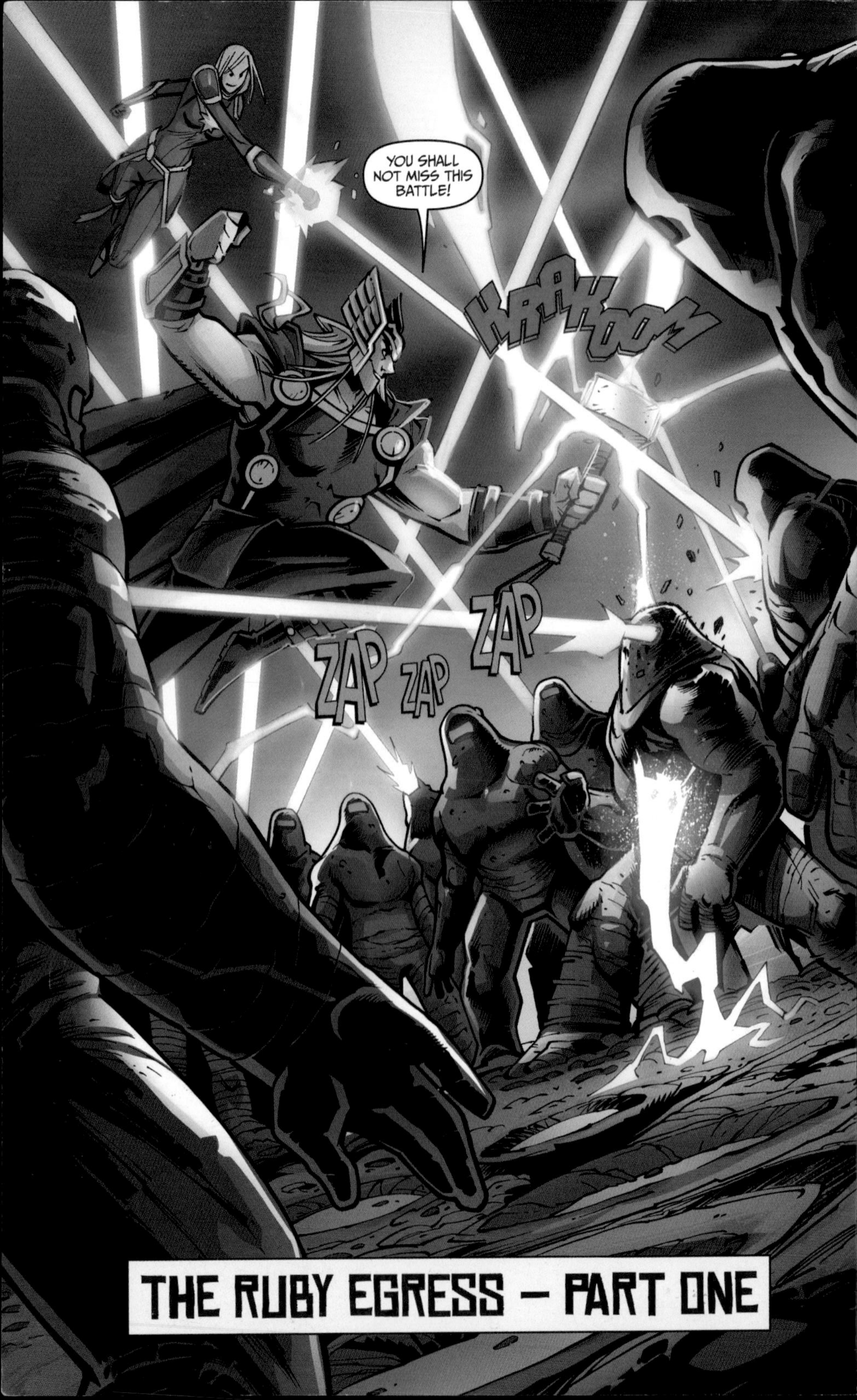
YOU SHALL NOT MISS THIS BATTLE!
KRAKOOM!
ZAP
ZAP
ZAP
THE RUBY EGRESS – PART ONE

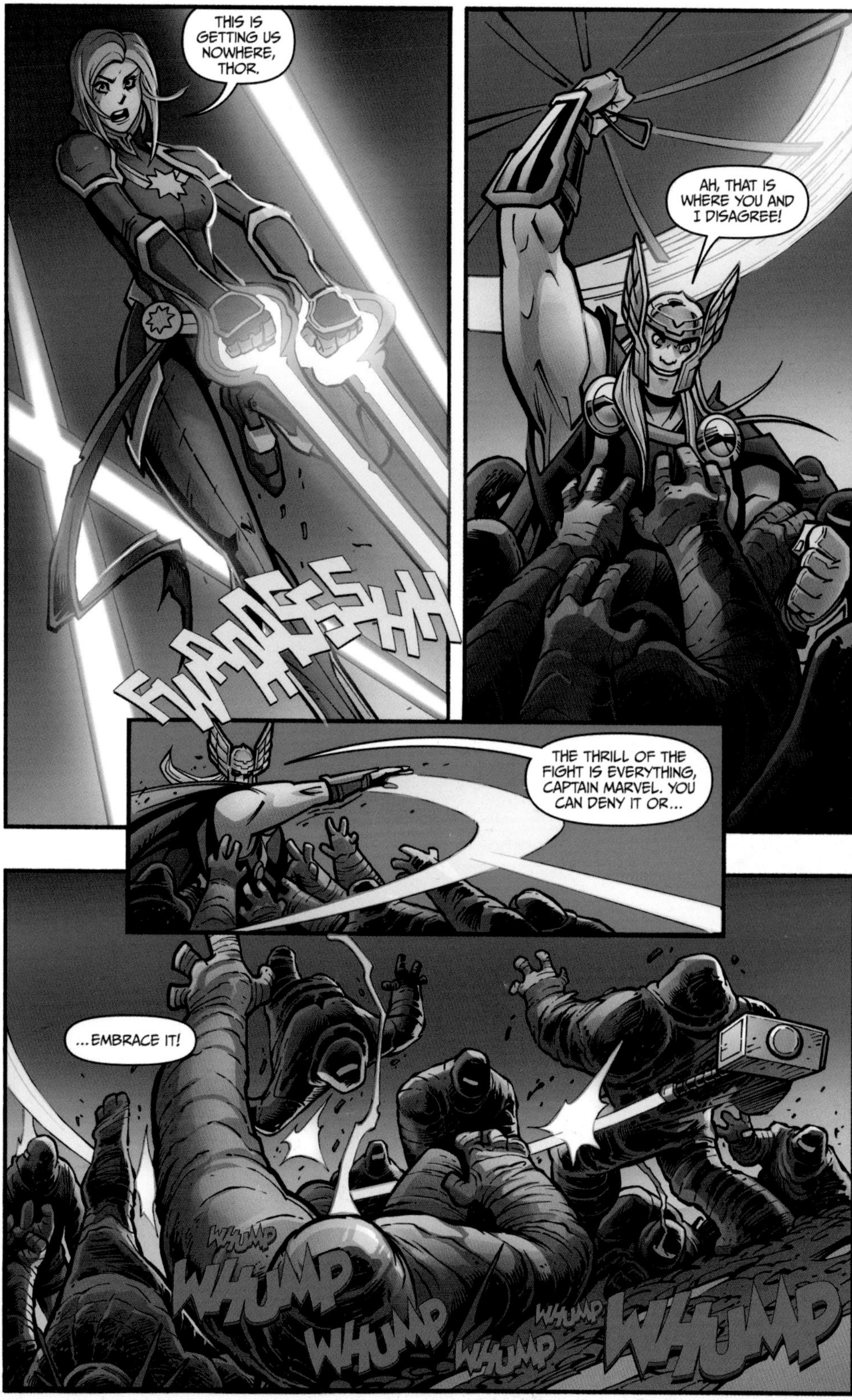
THIS IS GETTING US NOWHERE, THOR.
FWOOSSHH
AH, THAT IS WHERE YOU AND I DISAGREE!
THE THRILL OF THE FIGHT IS EVERYTHING, CAPTAIN MARVEL. YOU CAN DENY IT OR...
...EMBRACE IT!
WHUMP
WHUMP
WHUMP
WHUMP
WHUMP
WHUMP

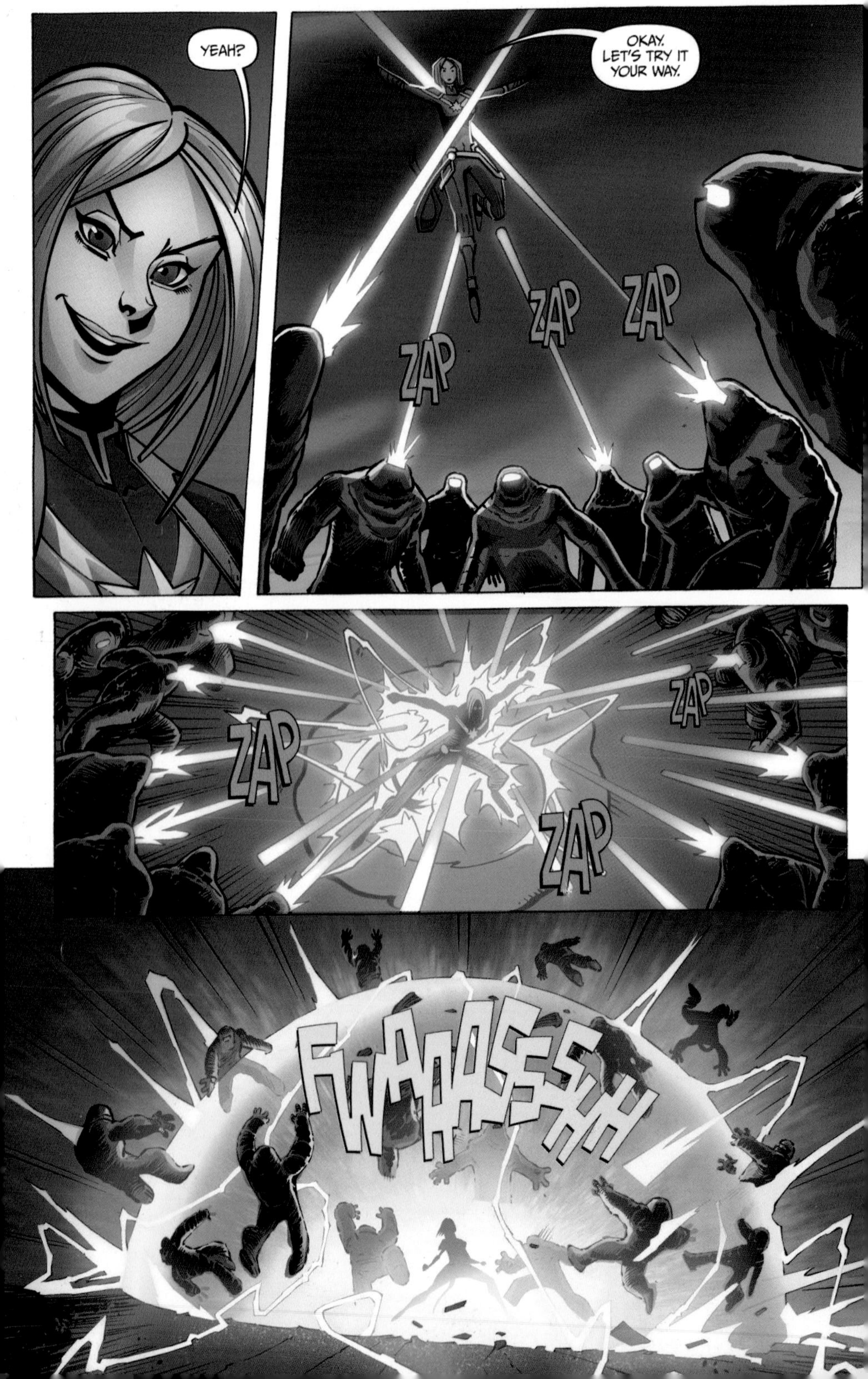
YEAH?
OKAY. LET'S TRY IT YOUR WAY.
ZAP
ZAP
ZAP
ZAP
ZAP
ZAP
FWAAOOSSHH

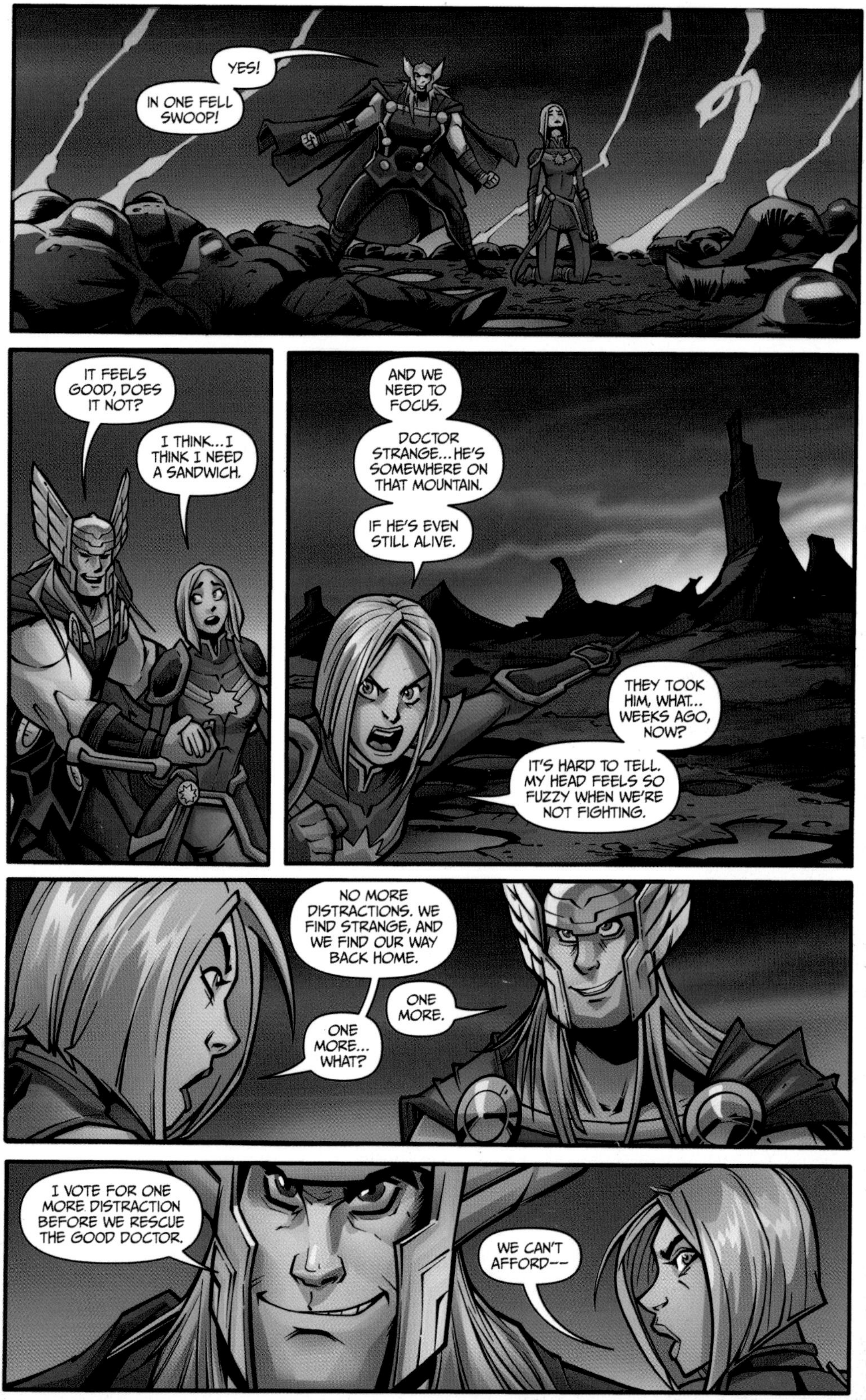
YES!
IN ONE FELL SWOOP!
IT FEELS GOOD, DOES IT NOT?
I THINK...I THINK I NEED A SANDWICH.
AND WE NEED TO FOCUS.
DOCTOR STRANGE...HE'S SOMEWHERE ON THAT MOUNTAIN.
IF HE'S EVEN STILL ALIVE.
THEY TOOK HIM, WHAT... WEEKS AGO, NOW?
IT'S HARD TO TELL. MY HEAD FEELS SO FUZZY WHEN WE'RE NOT FIGHTING.
NO MORE DISTRACTIONS. WE FIND STRANGE, AND WE FIND OUR WAY BACK HOME.
ONE MORE.
ONE MORE... WHAT?
I VOTE FOR ONE MORE DISTRACTION BEFORE WE RESCUE THE GOOD DOCTOR.
WE CAN'T AFFORD--

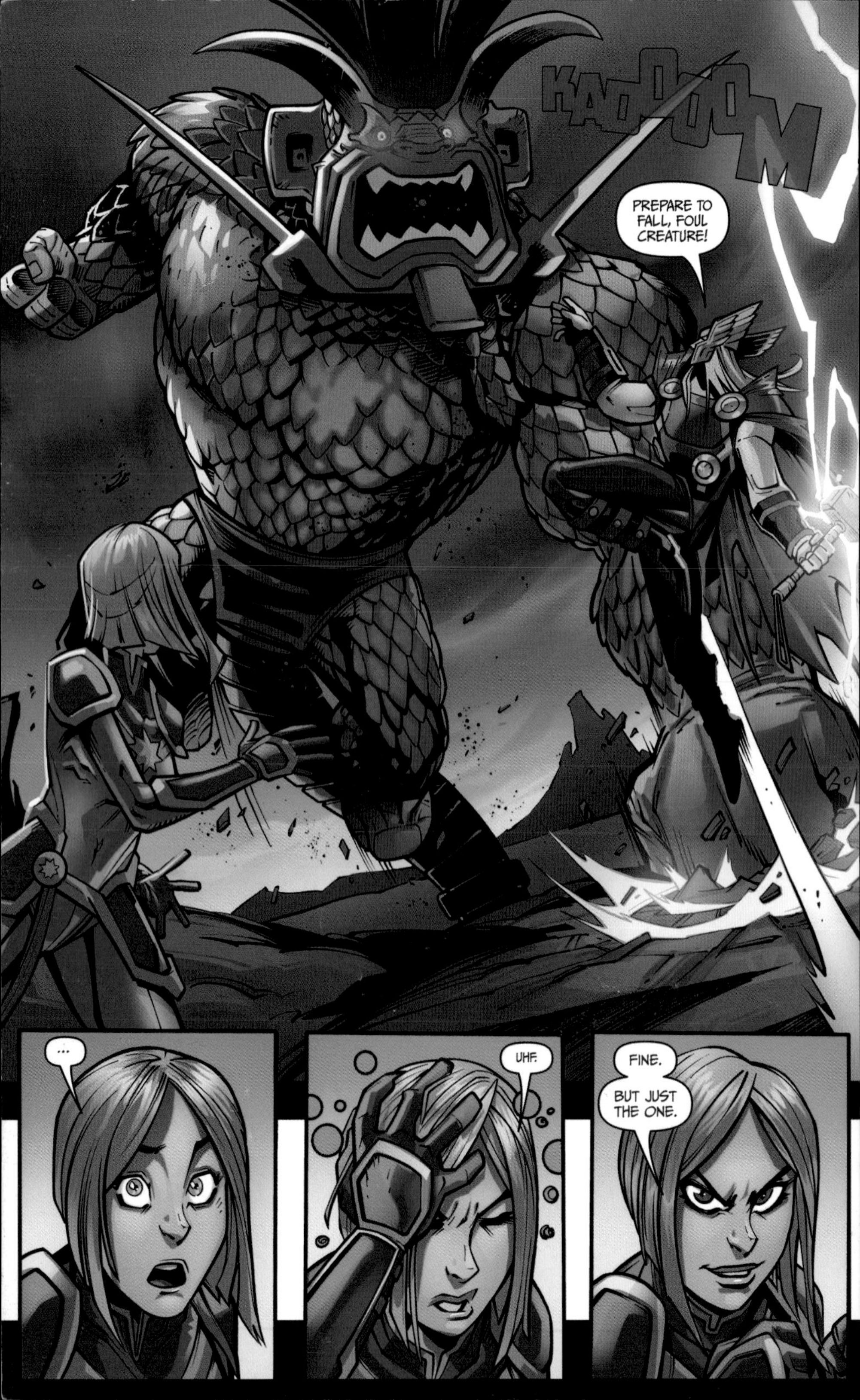
KADOOOOM
PREPARE TO FALL, FOUL CREATURE!
...
UHF.
FINE.
BUT JUST THE ONE.

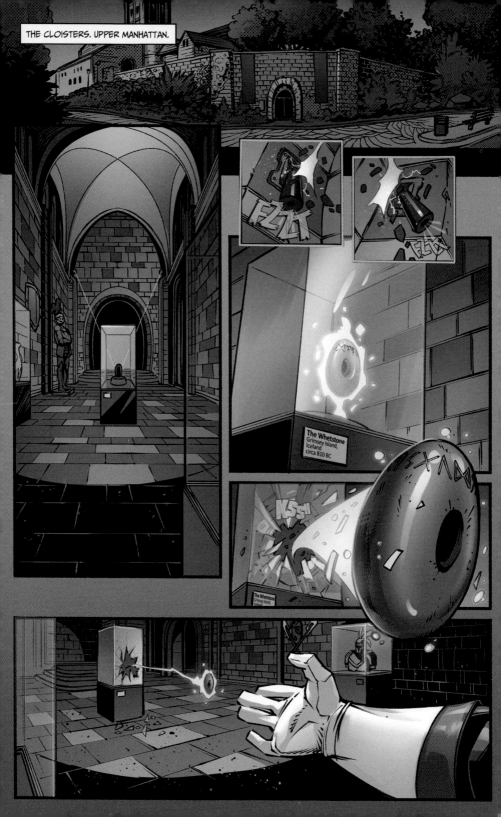

THE CLOISTERS. UPPER MANHATTAN.

The Whetstone
Grimsey Island,
Iceland
circa 810 BC

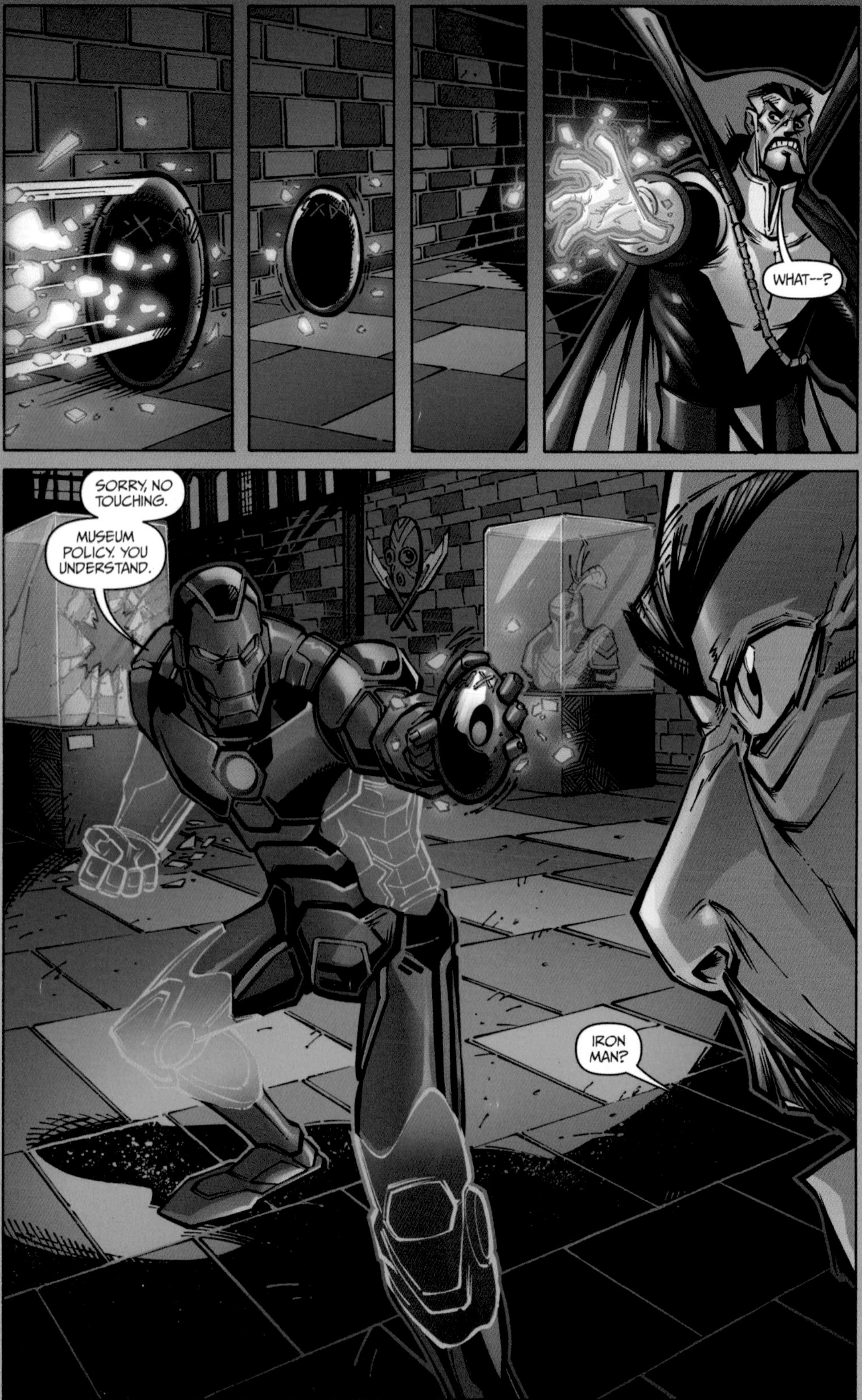
WHAT--?
SORRY, NO TOUCHING.
MUSEUM POLICY. YOU UNDERSTAND.
IRON MAN?

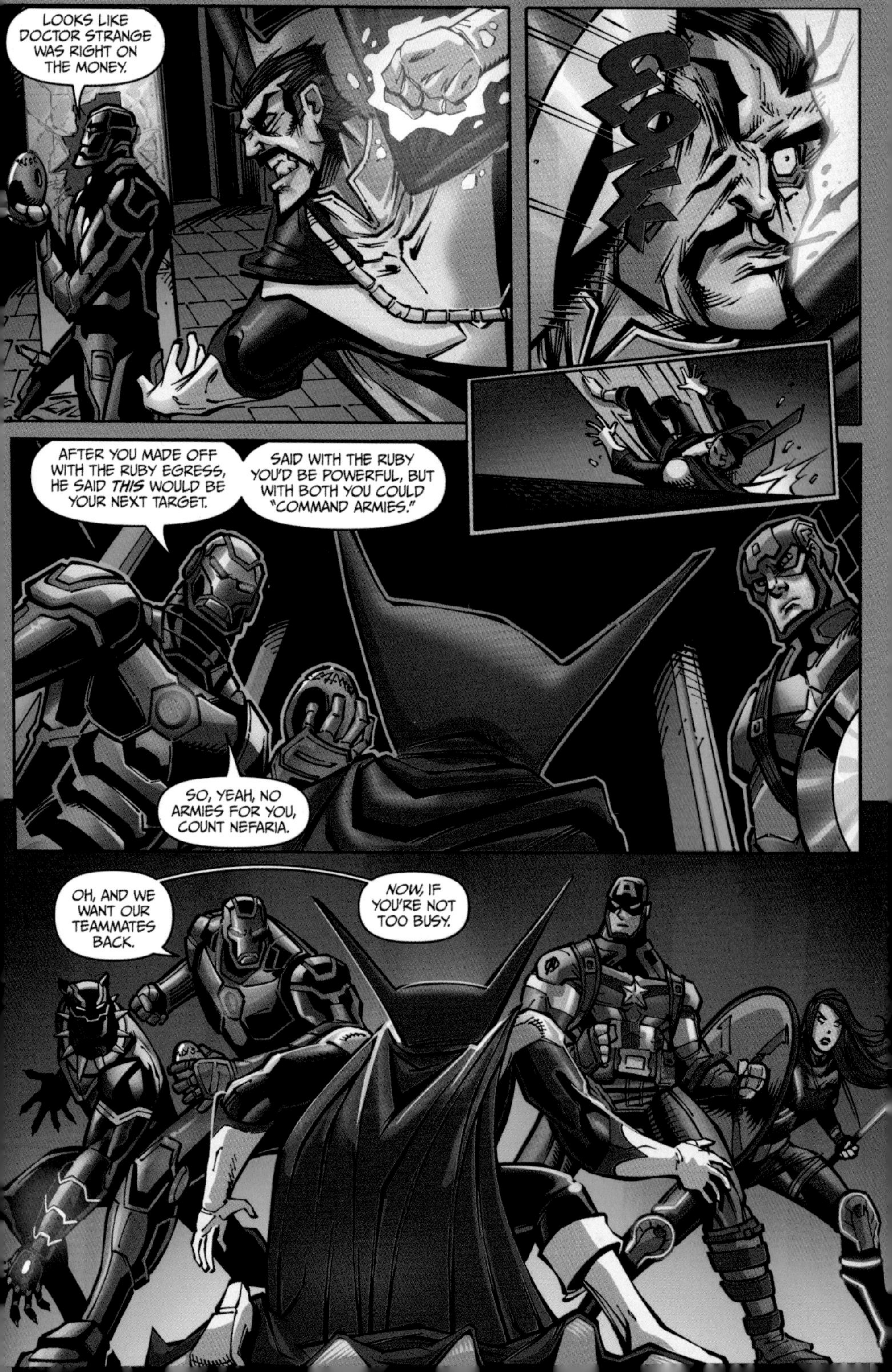
LOOKS LIKE DOCTOR STRANGE WAS RIGHT ON THE MONEY.
CLONK
AFTER YOU MADE OFF WITH THE RUBY EGRESS, HE SAID *THIS* WOULD BE YOUR NEXT TARGET.
SAID WITH THE RUBY YOU'D BE POWERFUL, BUT WITH BOTH YOU COULD "COMMAND ARMIES."
SO, YEAH, NO ARMIES FOR YOU, COUNT NEFARIA.
OH, AND WE WANT OUR TEAMMATES BACK.
NOW, IF YOU'RE NOT TOO BUSY.

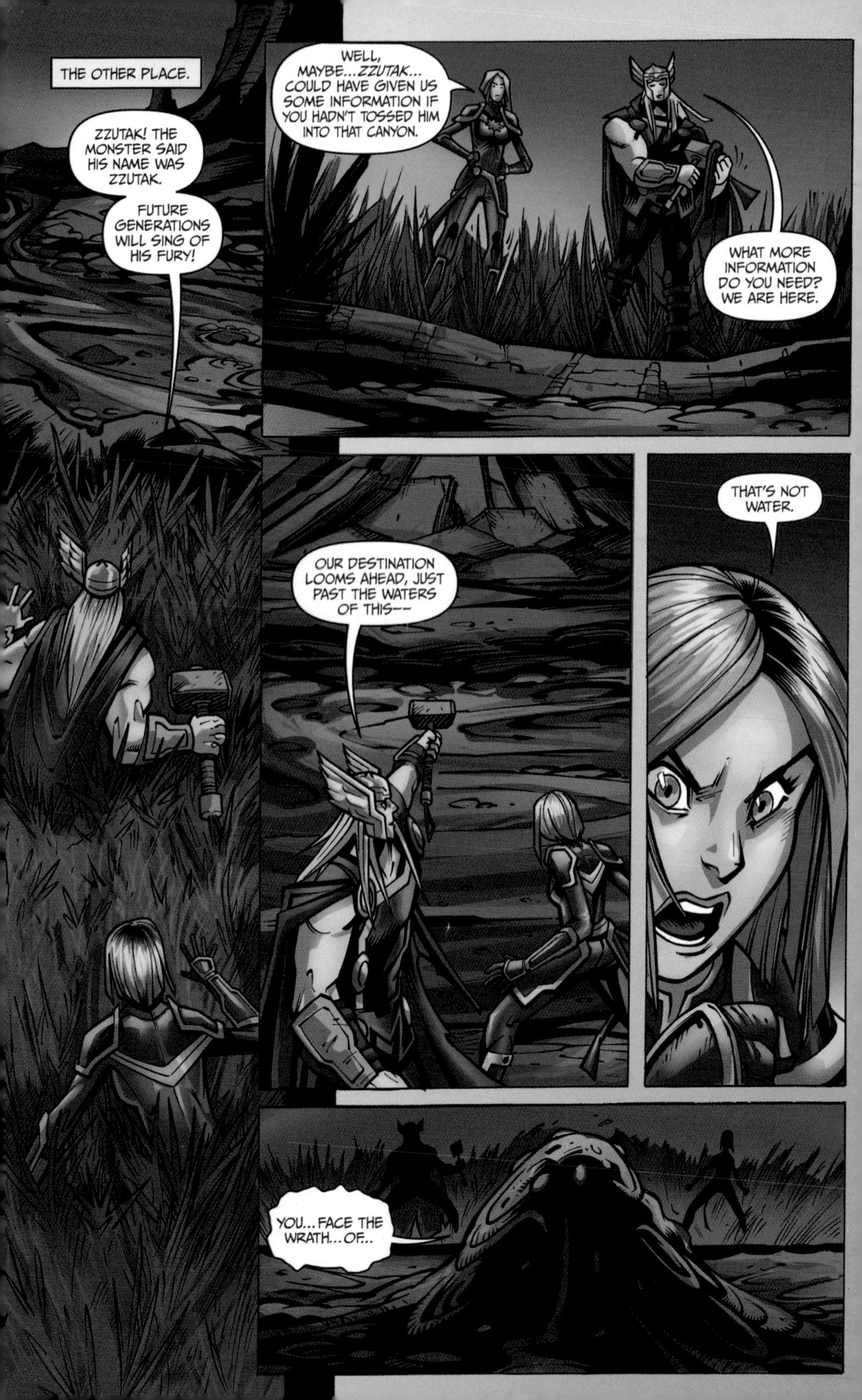

THE OTHER PLACE.
ZZUTAK! THE MONSTER SAID HIS NAME WAS ZZUTAK.
FUTURE GENERATIONS WILL SING OF HIS FURY!
WELL, MAYBE...ZZUTAK... COULD HAVE GIVEN US SOME INFORMATION IF YOU HADN'T TOSSED HIM INTO THAT CANYON.
WHAT MORE INFORMATION DO YOU NEED? WE ARE HERE.
OUR DESTINATION LOOMS AHEAD, JUST PAST THE WATERS OF THIS--
THAT'S NOT WATER.
YOU...FACE THE WRATH...OF..

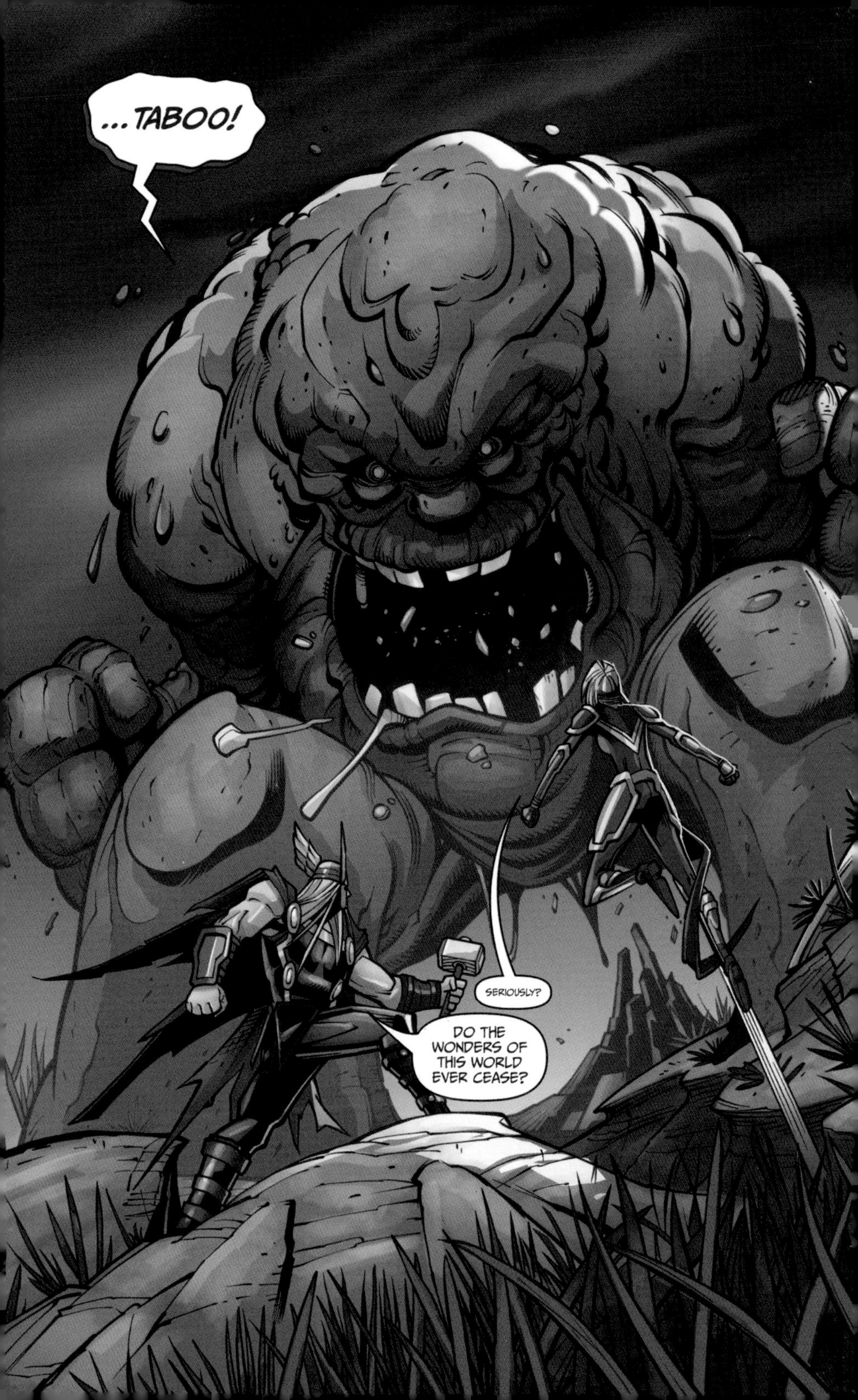
...TABOO!
SERIOUSLY?
DO THE WONDERS OF THIS WORLD EVER CEASE?

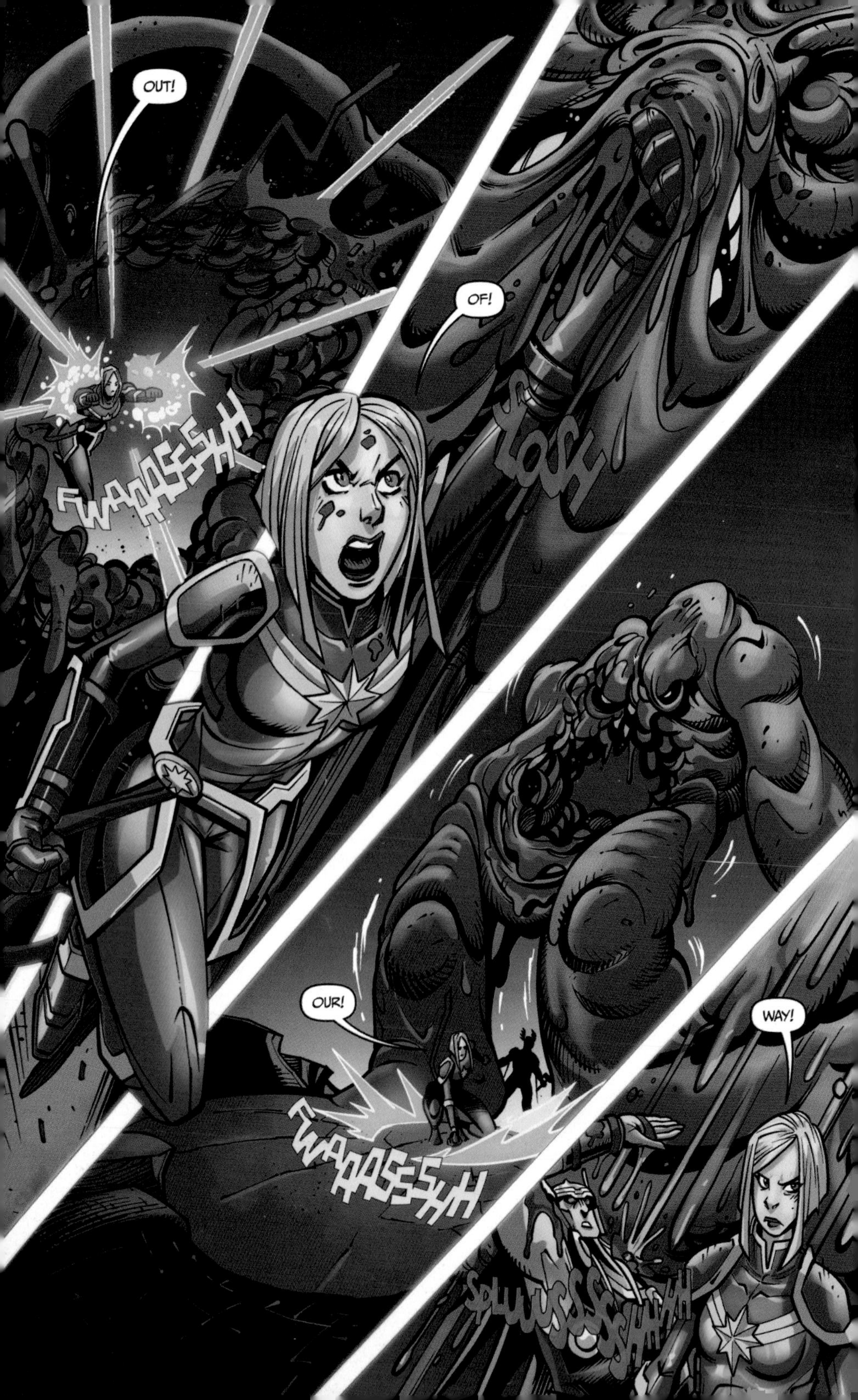
OUT!
FWAAASSSHH
OF!
ZASH
OUR!
FWAAASSSHH
WAY!
SPLUUSSSSHHH

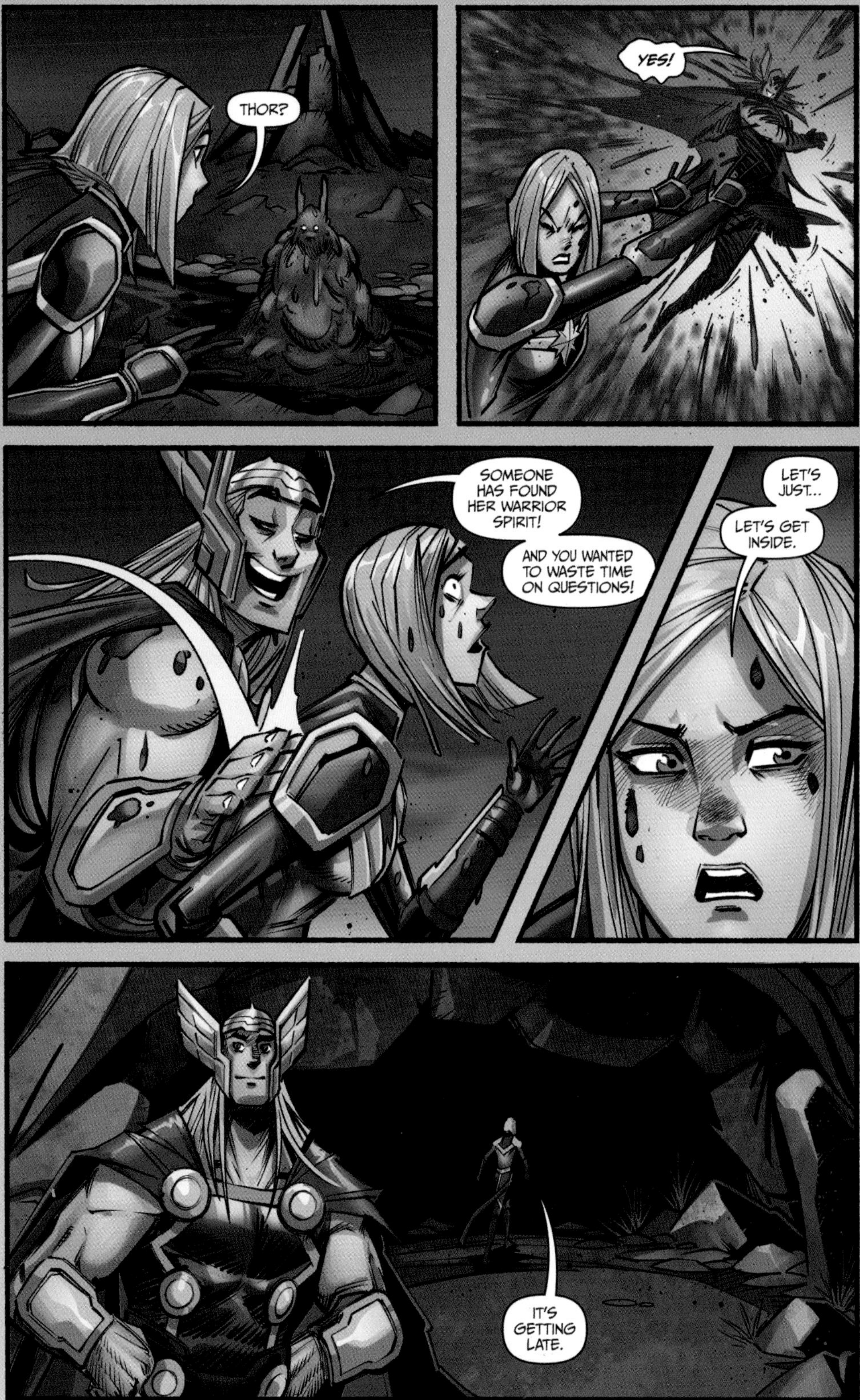
THOR?
YES!
SOMEONE HAS FOUND HER WARRIOR SPIRIT!
AND YOU WANTED TO WASTE TIME ON QUESTIONS!
LET'S JUST...
LET'S GET INSIDE.
IT'S GETTING LATE.

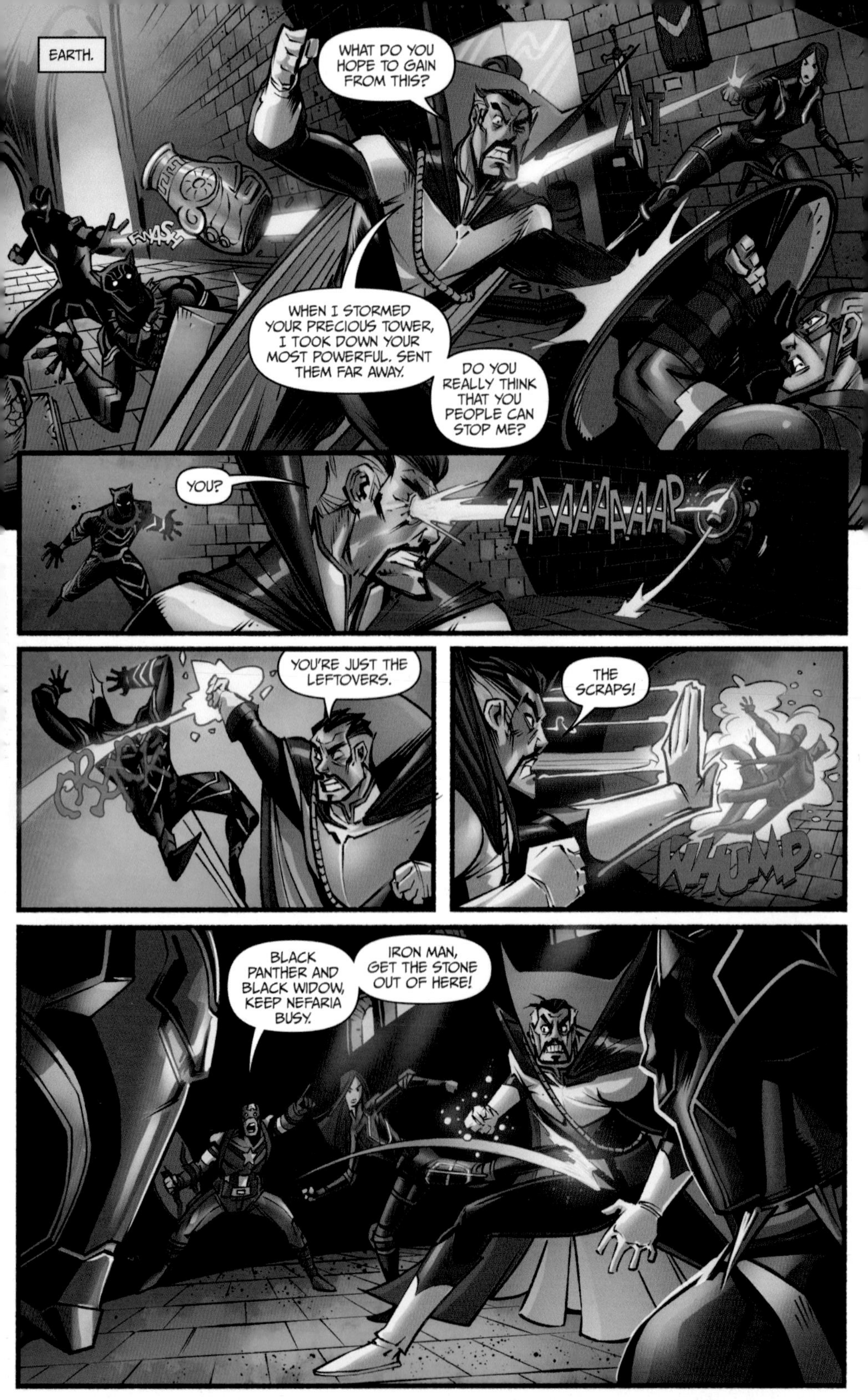
EARTH.
WHAT DO YOU HOPE TO GAIN FROM THIS?
ZAT
WHEN I STORMED YOUR PRECIOUS TOWER, I TOOK DOWN YOUR MOST POWERFUL. SENT THEM FAR AWAY.
DO YOU REALLY THINK THAT YOU PEOPLE CAN STOP ME?
YOU?
ZAAAAAAAP
YOU'RE JUST THE LEFTOVERS.
THE SCRAPS!
WHUMP
BLACK PANTHER AND BLACK WIDOW, KEEP NEFARIA BUSY.
IRON MAN, GET THE STONE OUT OF HERE!

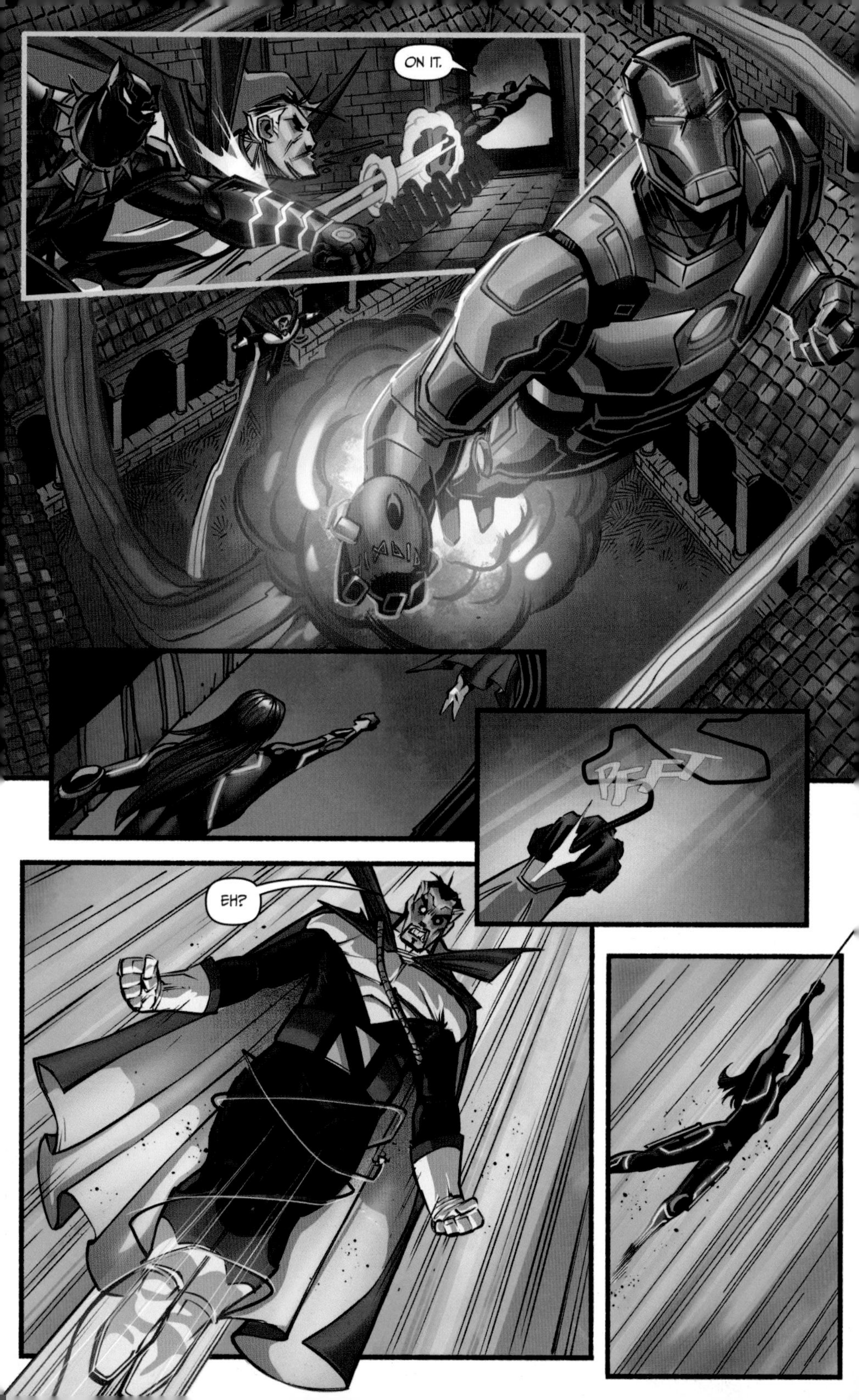
ON IT.
PFFT
EH?

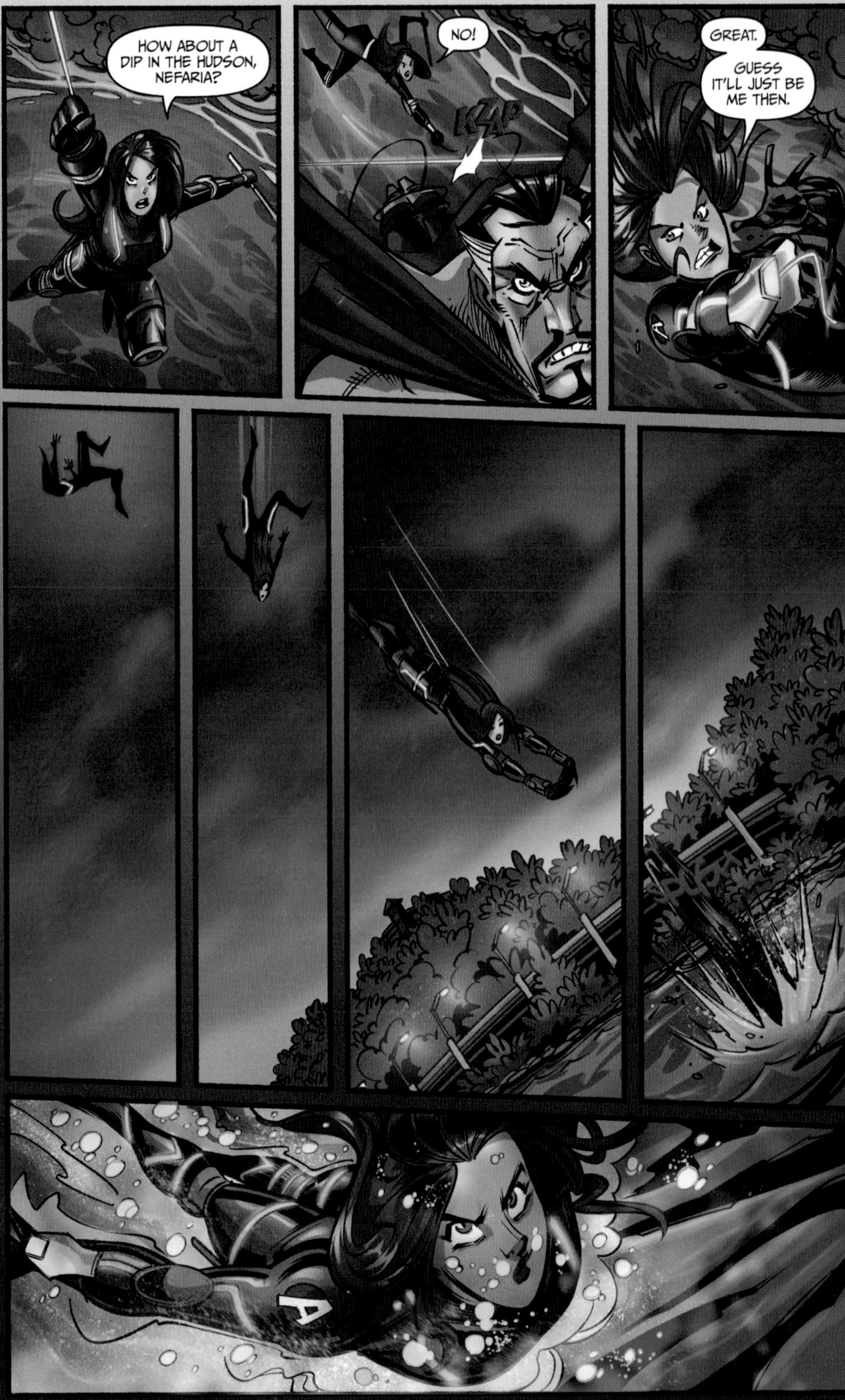
HOW ABOUT A DIP IN THE HUDSON, NEFARIA?
NO!
KZAP
GREAT.
GUESS IT'LL JUST BE ME THEN.

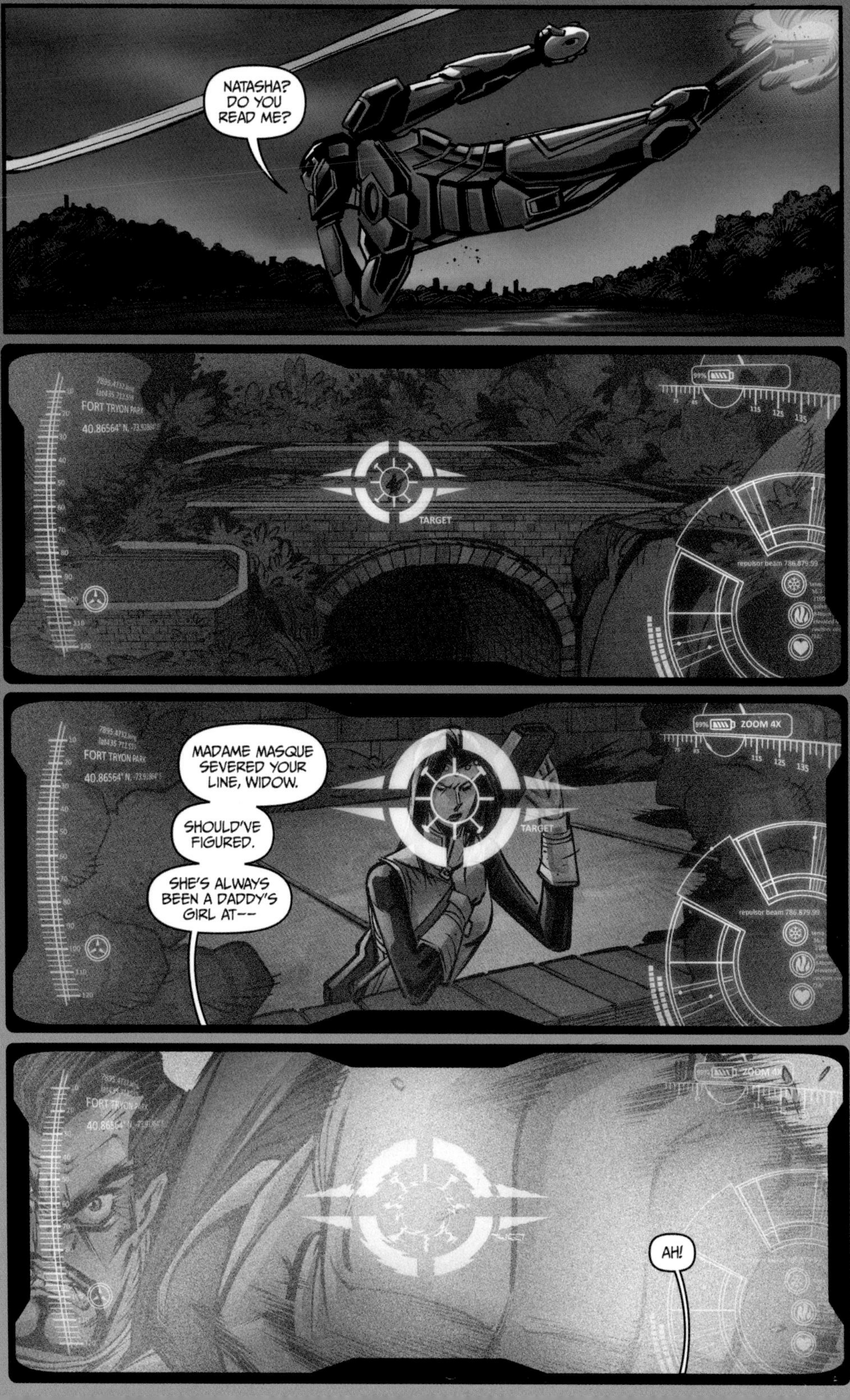
NATASHA? DO YOU READ ME?
FORT TRYON PARK
40.86564° N, -73.93845°
99%
TARGET
repulsor beam 786.879.99
FORT TRYON PARK
99%
ZOOM 4X
MADAME MASQUE SEVERED YOUR LINE, WIDOW.
SHOULD'VE FIGURED.
SHE'S ALWAYS BEEN A DADDY'S GIRL AT--
TARGET
repulsor beam 786.879.99
AH!

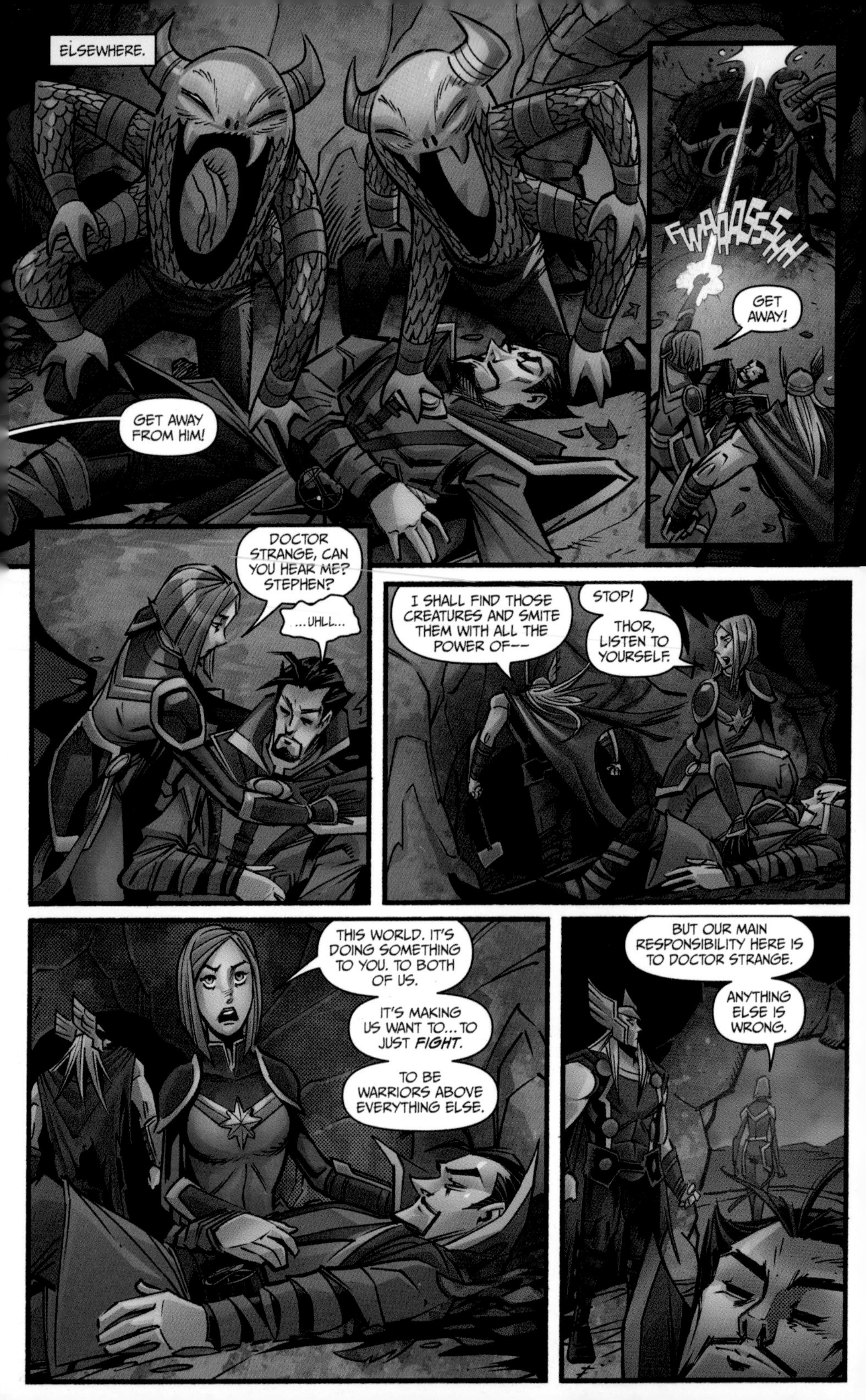
ELSEWHERE.
GET AWAY FROM HIM!
FWOOOSSHH
GET AWAY!
DOCTOR STRANGE, CAN YOU HEAR ME? STEPHEN?
...UHLL...
I SHALL FIND THOSE CREATURES AND SMITE THEM WITH ALL THE POWER OF--
STOP!
THOR, LISTEN TO YOURSELF.
THIS WORLD. IT'S DOING SOMETHING TO YOU. TO BOTH OF US.
IT'S MAKING US WANT TO... TO JUST FIGHT.
TO BE WARRIORS ABOVE EVERYTHING ELSE.
BUT OUR MAIN RESPONSIBILITY HERE IS TO DOCTOR STRANGE.
ANYTHING ELSE IS WRONG.

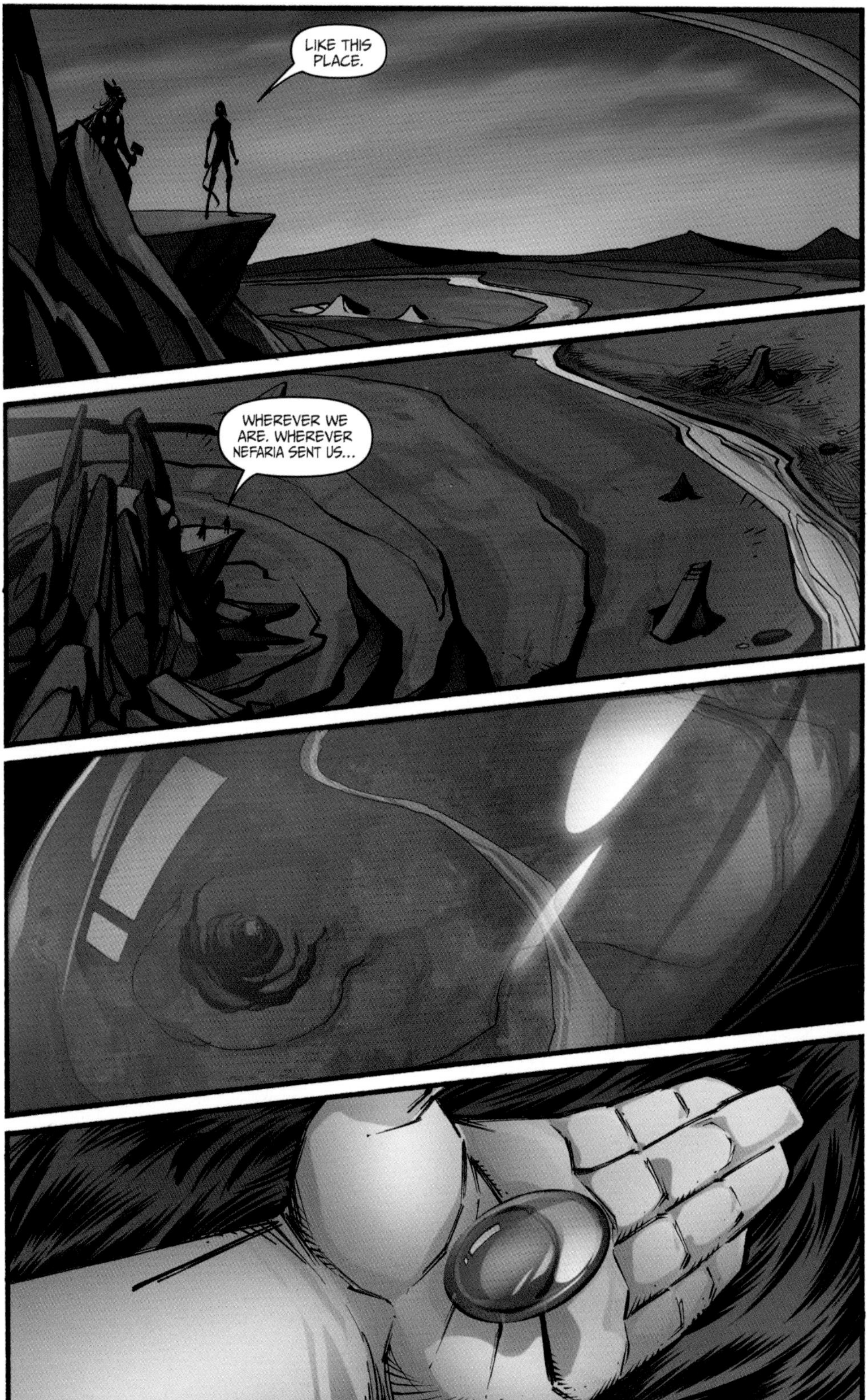
LIKE THIS PLACE.
WHEREVER WE ARE. WHEREVER NEFARIA SENT US...

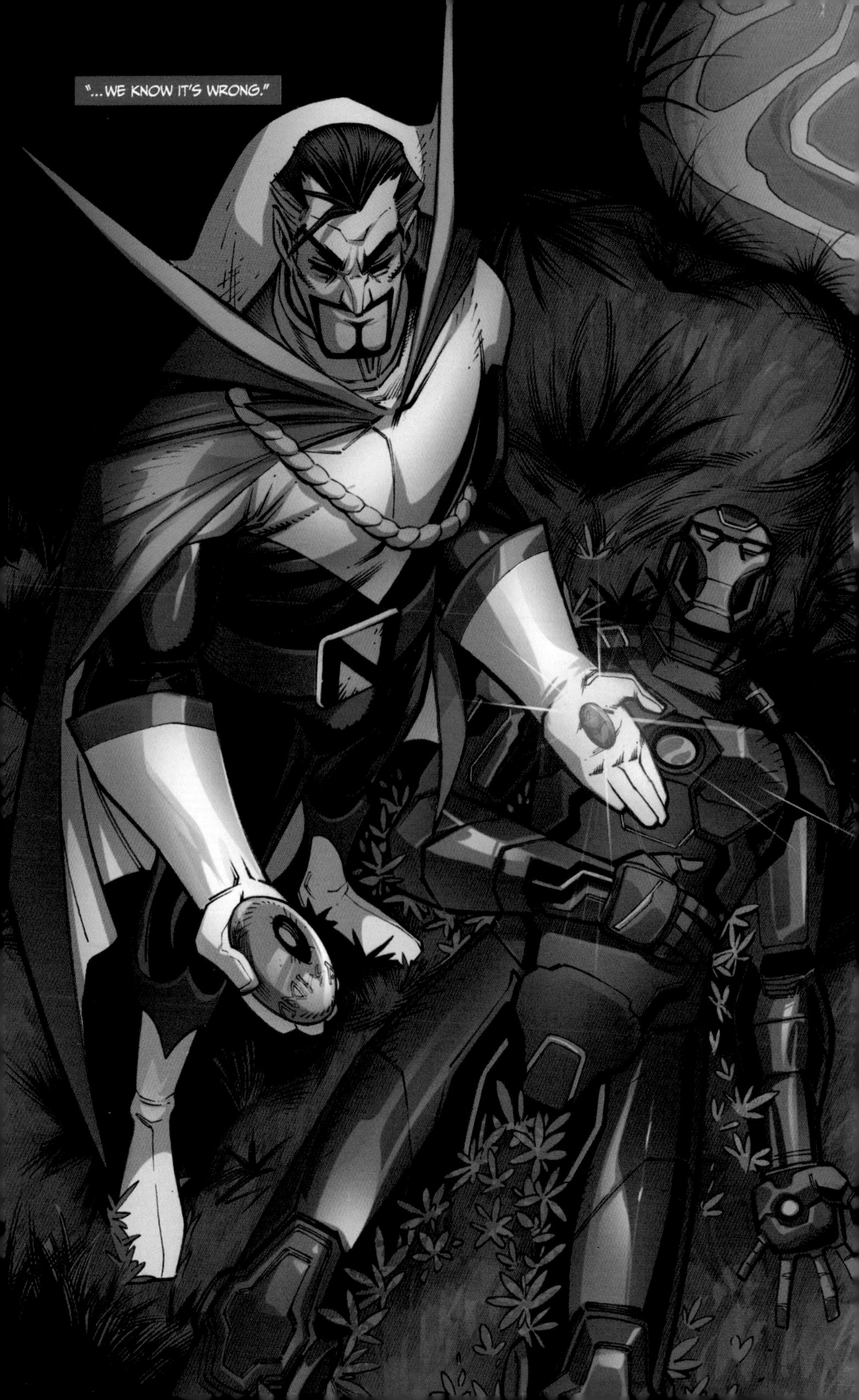
"...WE KNOW IT'S WRONG."

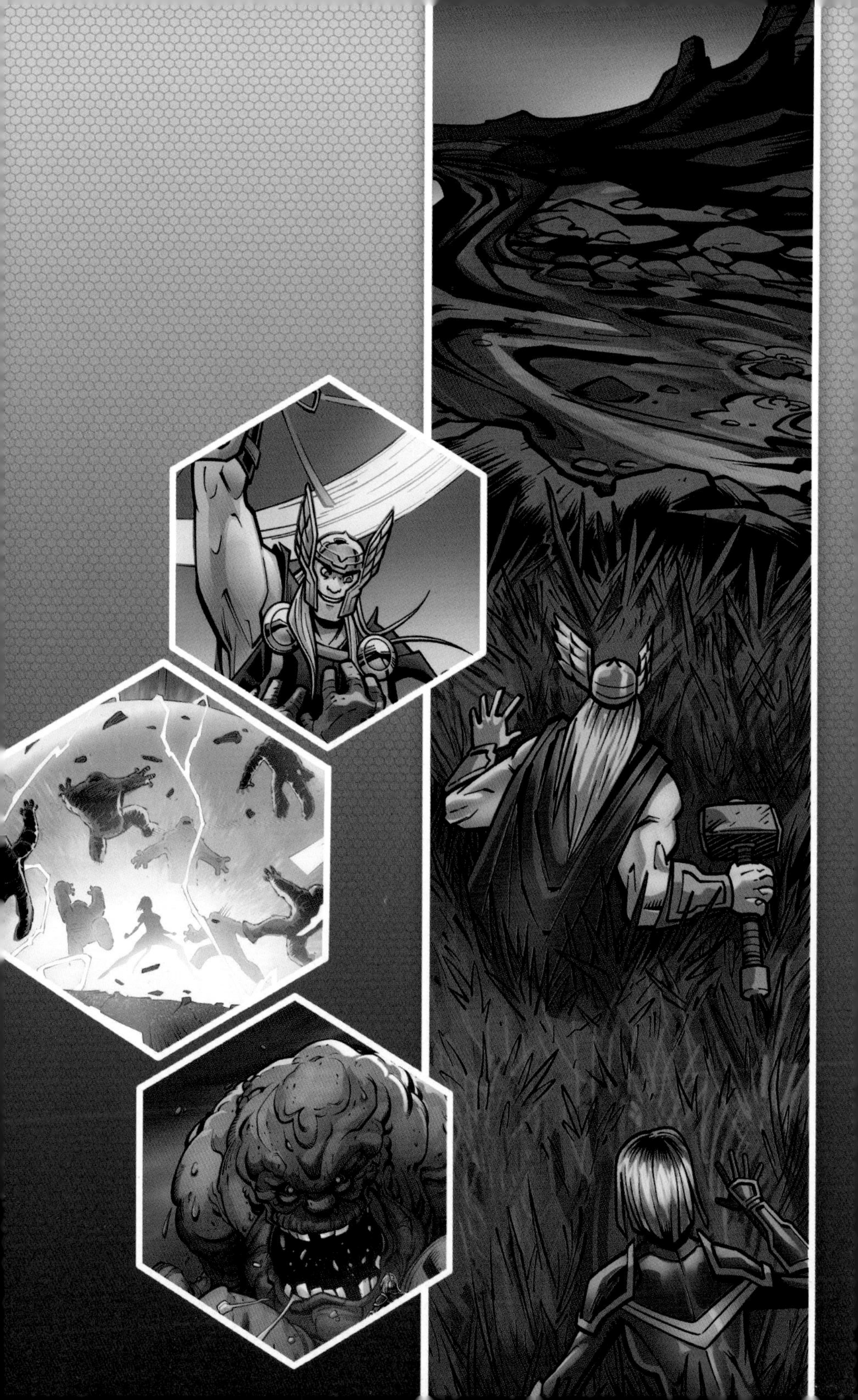

ART BY: JON SOMMARIVA

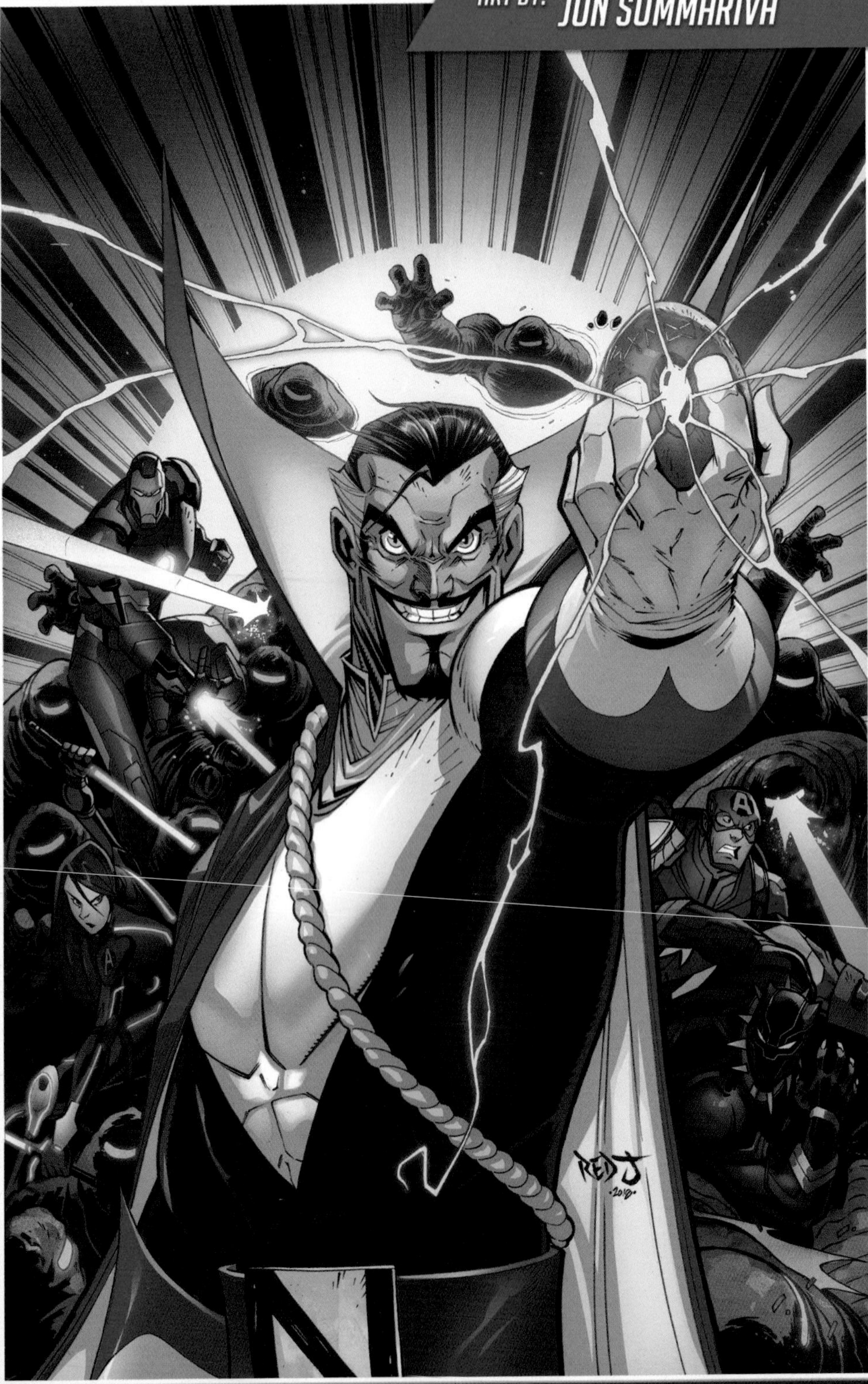

RED J
2018

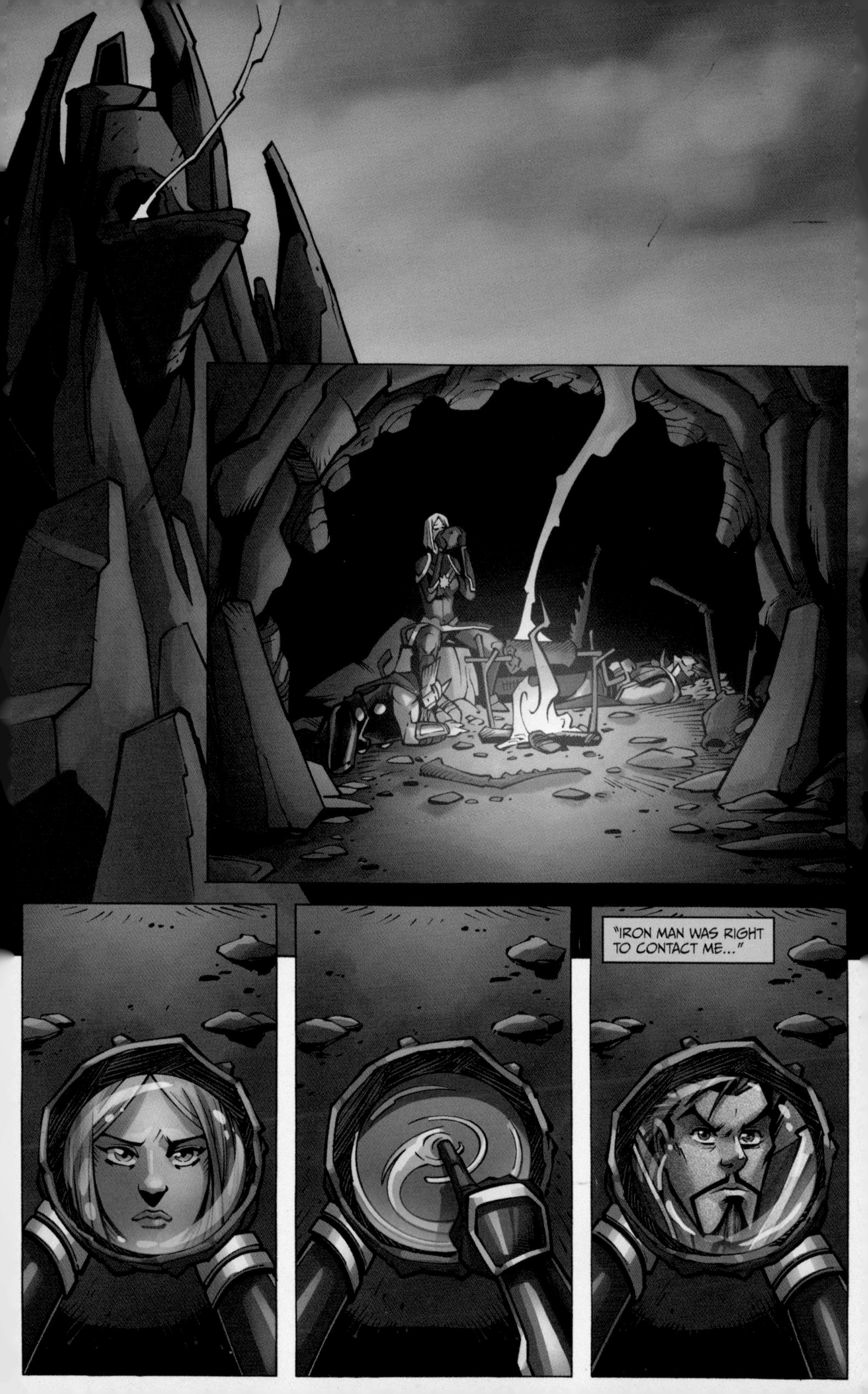
"IRON MAN WAS RIGHT TO CONTACT ME..."

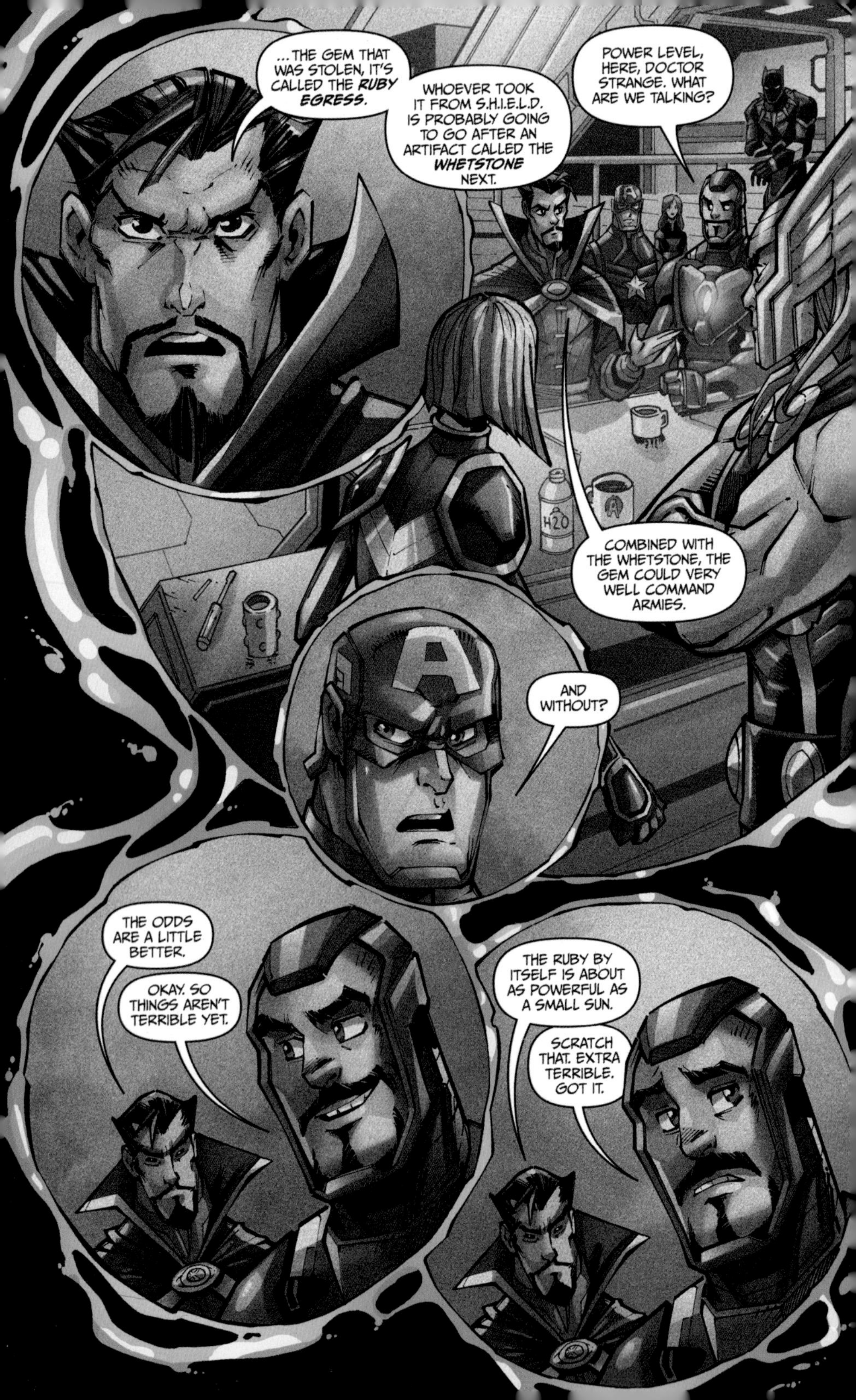

...THE GEM THAT WAS STOLEN, IT'S CALLED THE RUBY EGRESS.
WHOEVER TOOK IT FROM S.H.I.E.L.D. IS PROBABLY GOING TO GO AFTER AN ARTIFACT CALLED THE WHETSTONE NEXT.
POWER LEVEL, HERE, DOCTOR STRANGE. WHAT ARE WE TALKING?
COMBINED WITH THE WHETSTONE, THE GEM COULD VERY WELL COMMAND ARMIES.
AND WITHOUT?
THE ODDS ARE A LITTLE BETTER.
OKAY. SO THINGS AREN'T TERRIBLE YET.
THE RUBY BY ITSELF IS ABOUT AS POWERFUL AS A SMALL SUN.
SCRATCH THAT. EXTRA TERRIBLE. GOT IT.

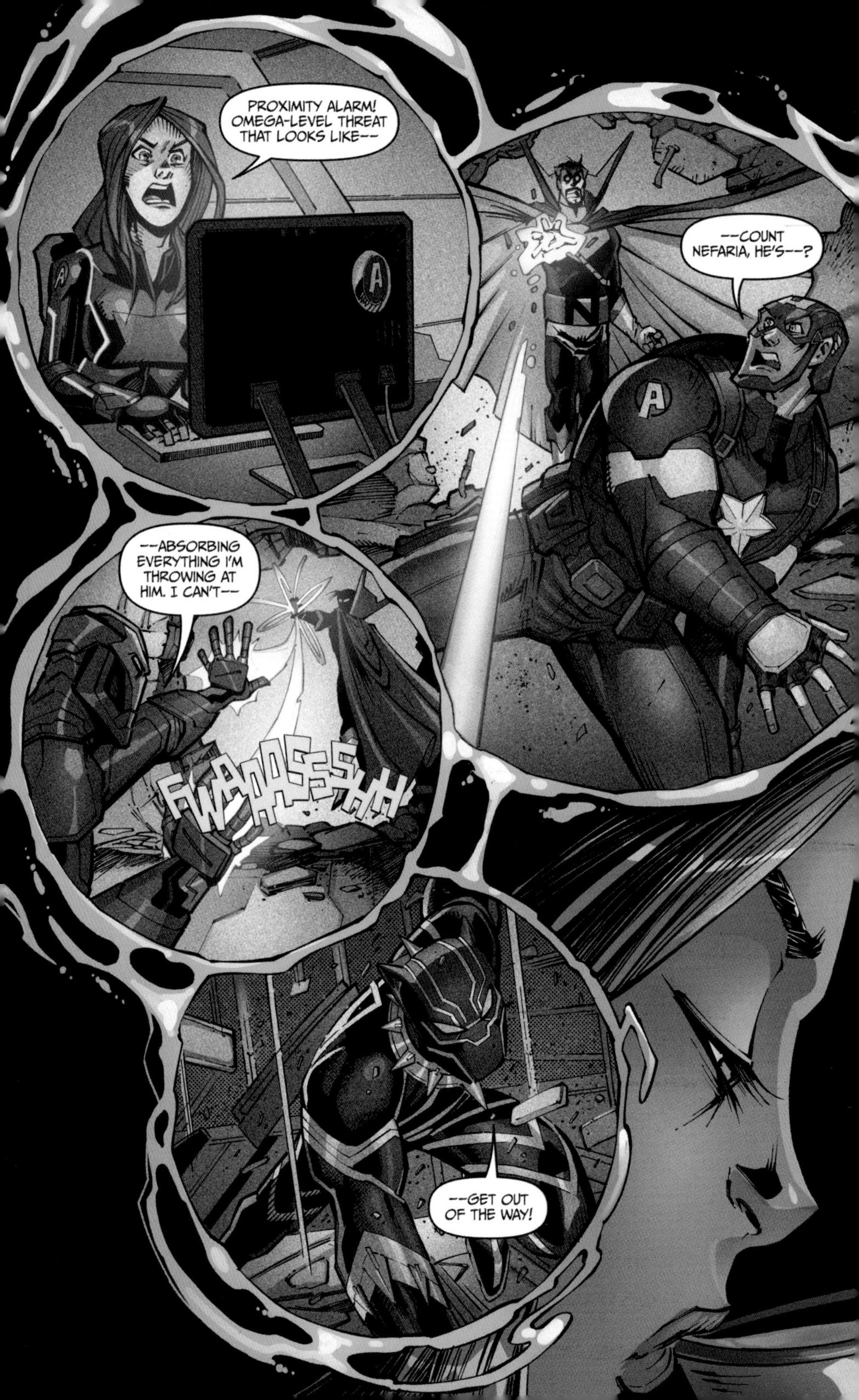
PROXIMITY ALARM! OMEGA-LEVEL THREAT THAT LOOKS LIKE--
--COUNT NEFARIA, HE'S--?
--ABSORBING EVERYTHING I'M THROWING AT HIM. I CAN'T--
FWOOSSSHH
--GET OUT OF THE WAY!

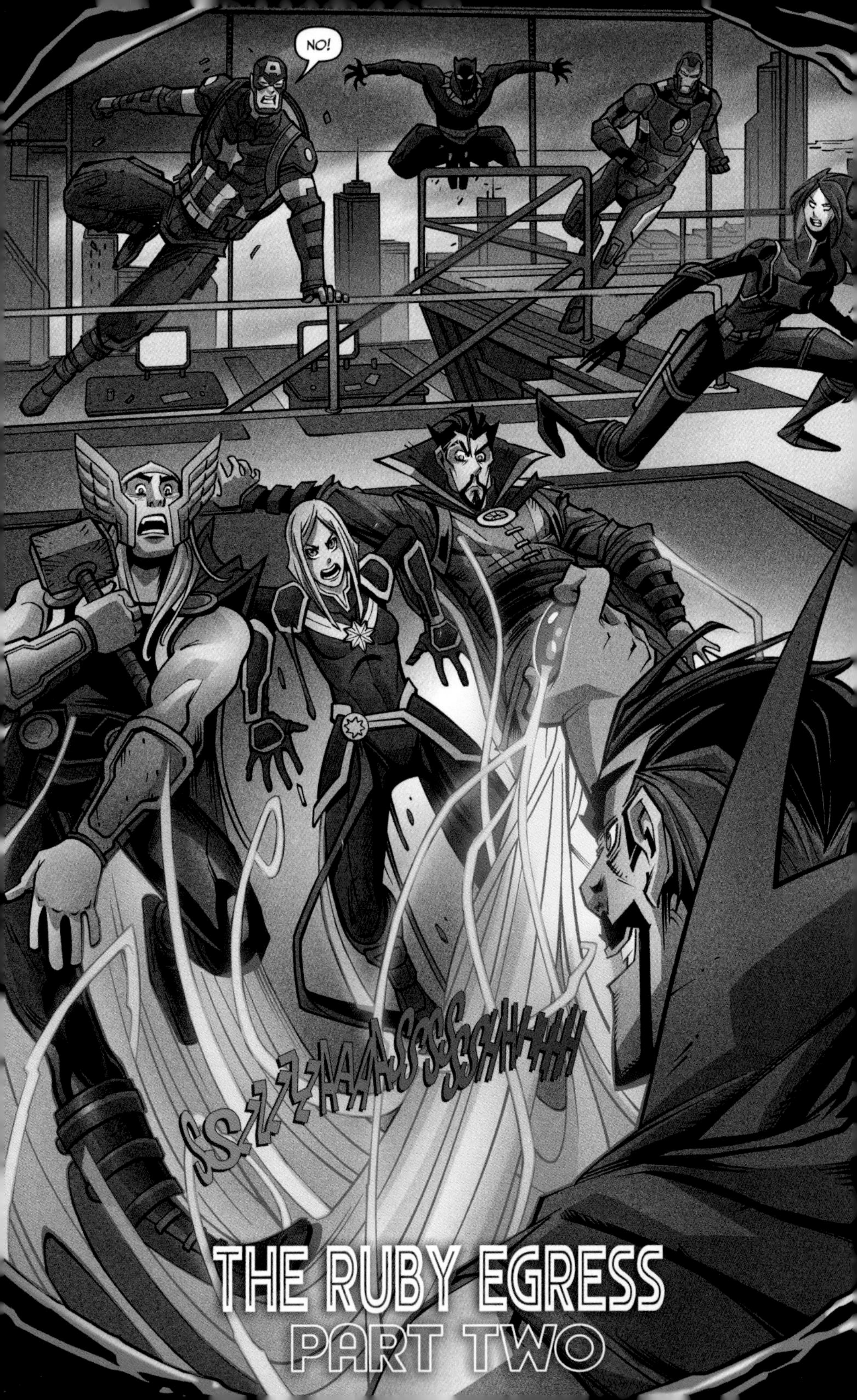
NO!
SSZZZZHAAAASSSSSHHHHH
THE RUBY EGRESS
PART TWO

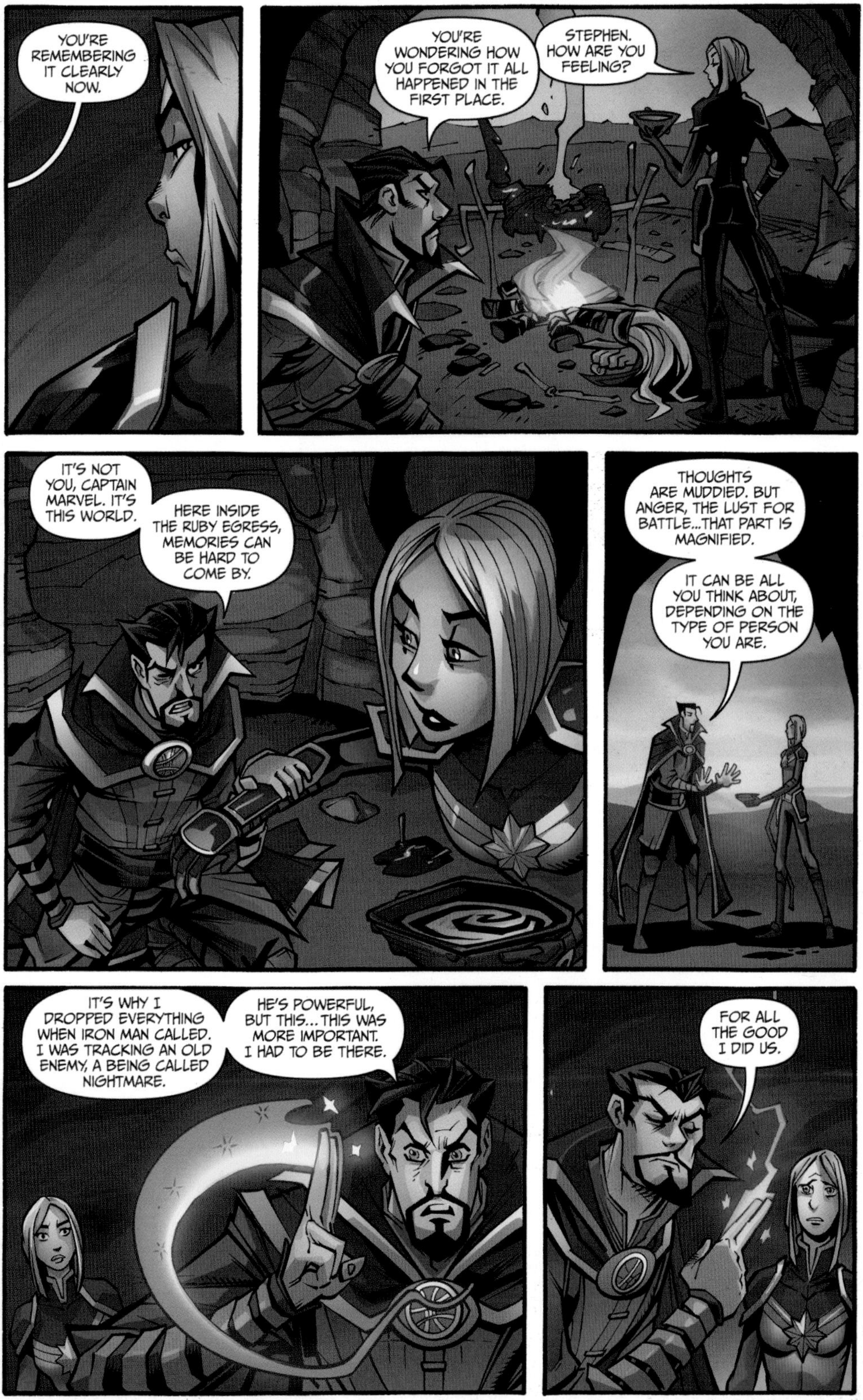
YOU'RE REMEMBERING IT CLEARLY NOW.
YOU'RE WONDERING HOW YOU FORGOT IT ALL HAPPENED IN THE FIRST PLACE.
STEPHEN. HOW ARE YOU FEELING?
IT'S NOT YOU, CAPTAIN MARVEL. IT'S THIS WORLD.
HERE INSIDE THE RUBY EGRESS, MEMORIES CAN BE HARD TO COME BY.
THOUGHTS ARE MUDDIED. BUT ANGER, THE LUST FOR BATTLE...THAT PART IS MAGNIFIED.
IT CAN BE ALL YOU THINK ABOUT, DEPENDING ON THE TYPE OF PERSON YOU ARE.
IT'S WHY I DROPPED EVERYTHING WHEN IRON MAN CALLED. I WAS TRACKING AN OLD ENEMY, A BEING CALLED NIGHTMARE.
HE'S POWERFUL, BUT THIS...THIS WAS MORE IMPORTANT. I HAD TO BE THERE.
FOR ALL THE GOOD I DID US.

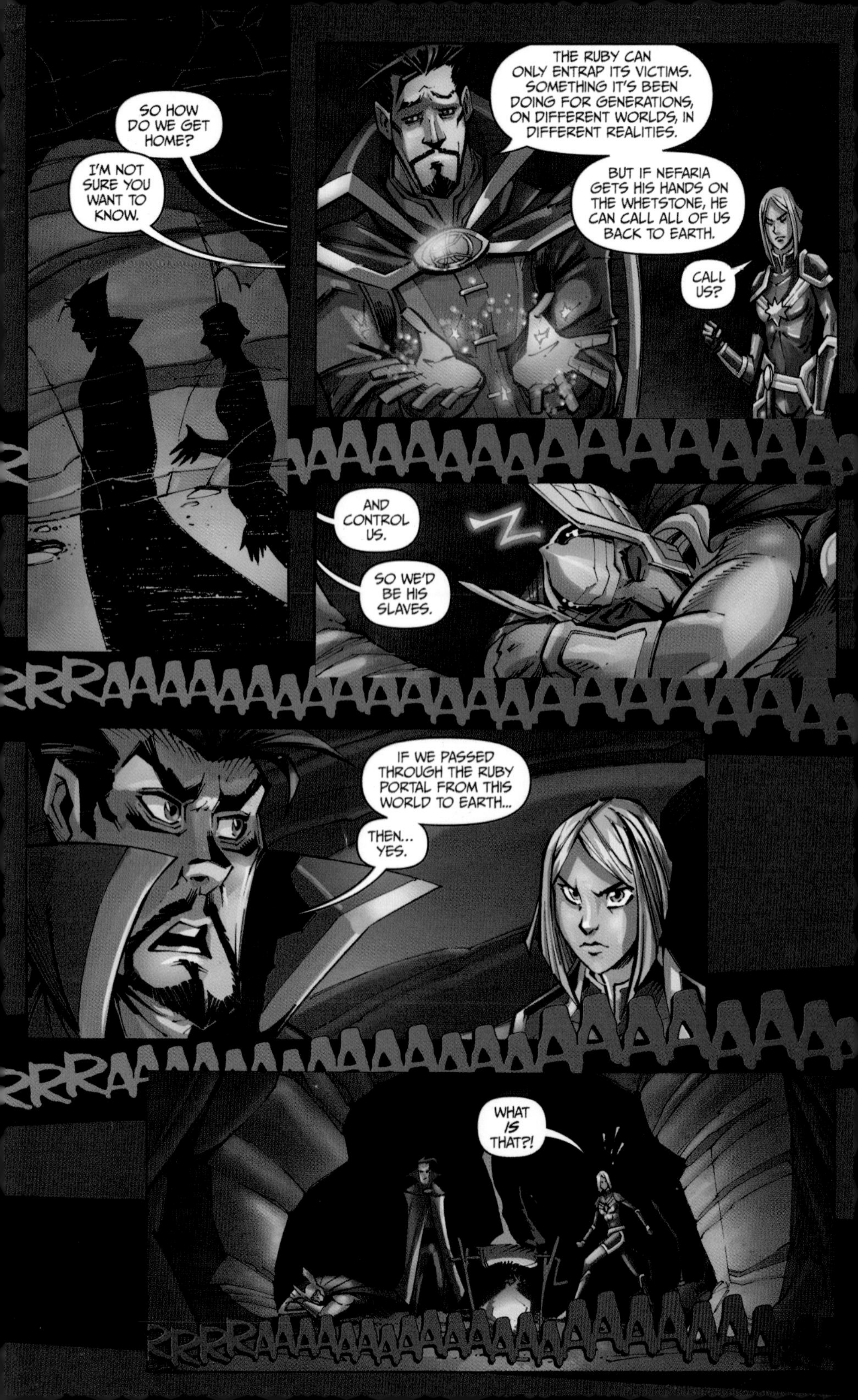

SO HOW DO WE GET HOME?
I'M NOT SURE YOU WANT TO KNOW.
THE RUBY CAN ONLY ENTRAP ITS VICTIMS. SOMETHING IT'S BEEN DOING FOR GENERATIONS, ON DIFFERENT WORLDS, IN DIFFERENT REALITIES.
BUT IF NEFARIA GETS HIS HANDS ON THE WHETSTONE, HE CAN CALL ALL OF US BACK TO EARTH.
CALL US?
RRAAAAAAAAAAAAAAAAAA
AND CONTROL US.
SO WE'D BE HIS SLAVES.
RRRAAAAAAAAAAAAAAAAAAAAAAAAA
IF WE PASSED THROUGH THE RUBY PORTAL FROM THIS WORLD TO EARTH...
THEN... YES.
RRRAAAAAAAAAAAAAAAAAAAAA
WHAT IS THAT?!
RRRRAAAAAAAAAAAAAAAAAAAAA

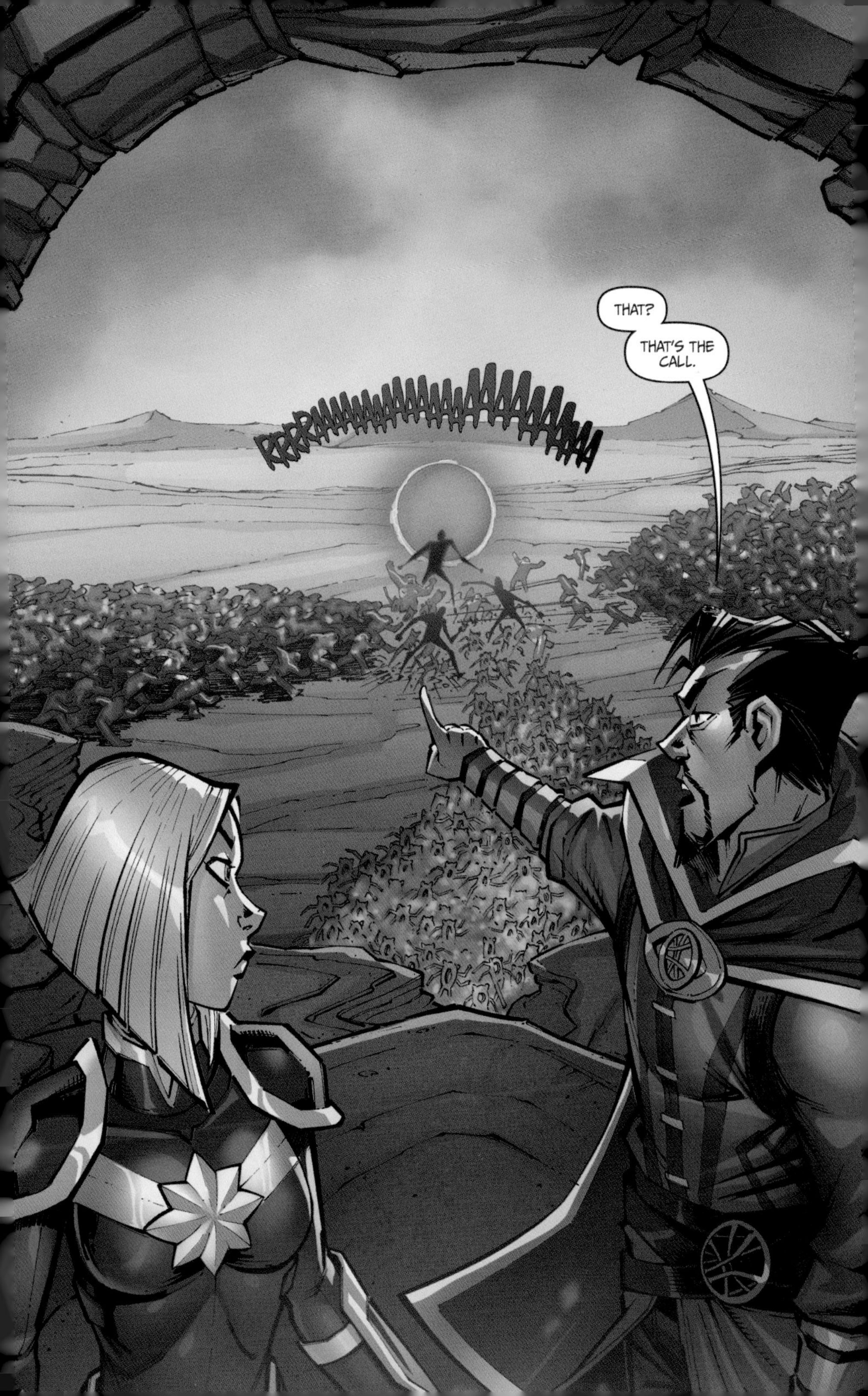
THAT?
THAT'S THE CALL.

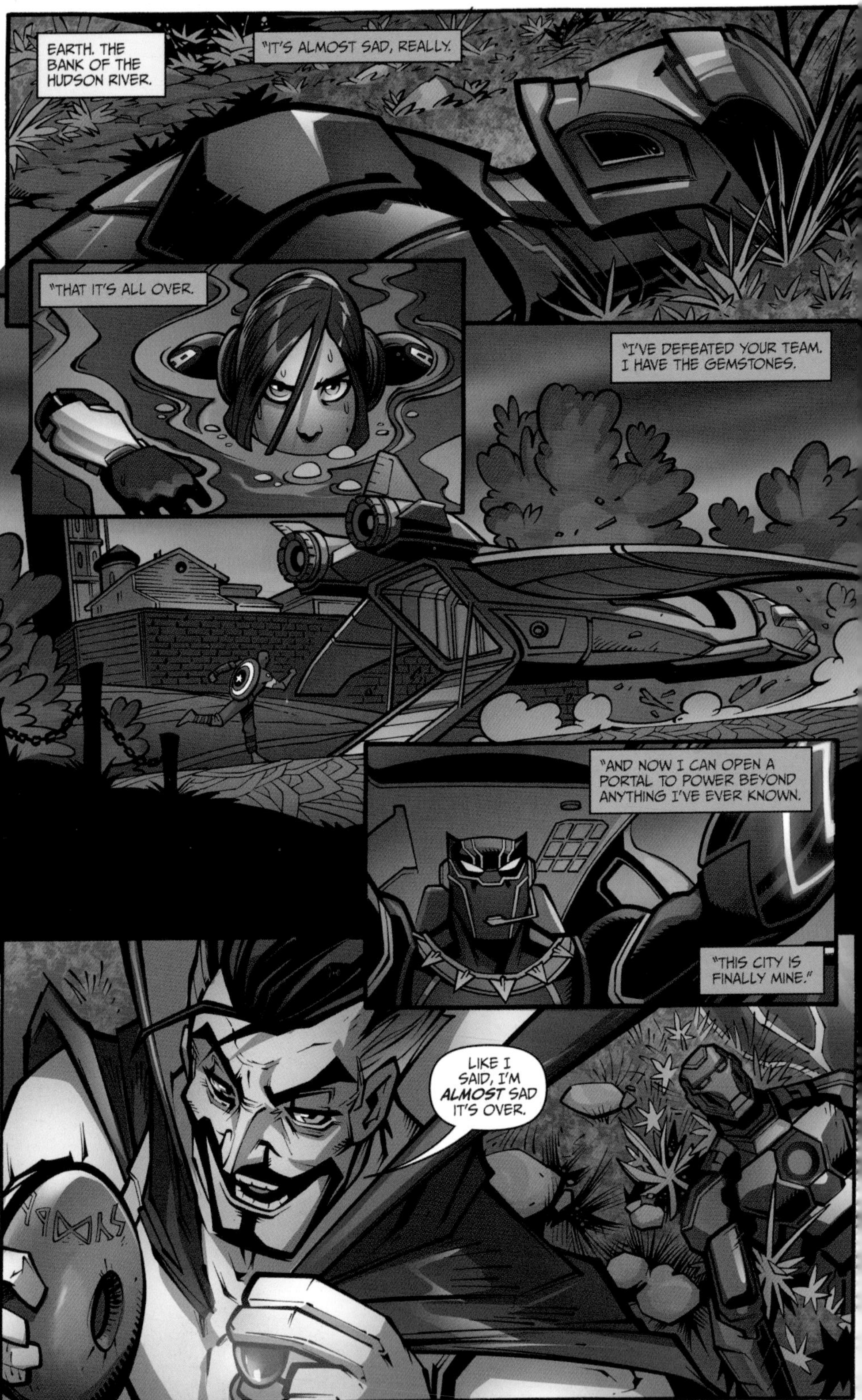
EARTH. THE BANK OF THE HUDSON RIVER.
"IT'S ALMOST SAD, REALLY.
"THAT IT'S ALL OVER.
"I'VE DEFEATED YOUR TEAM. I HAVE THE GEMSTONES.
"AND NOW I CAN OPEN A PORTAL TO POWER BEYOND ANYTHING I'VE EVER KNOWN.
"THIS CITY IS FINALLY MINE."
LIKE I SAID, I'M ALMOST SAD IT'S OVER.

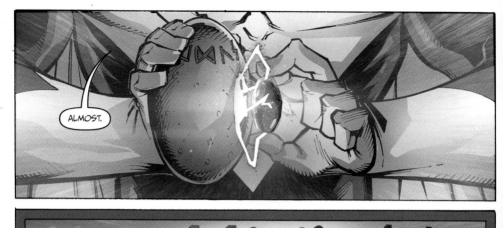

ALMOST.

SSZZZZAAAASSSSSSsHHHHHH

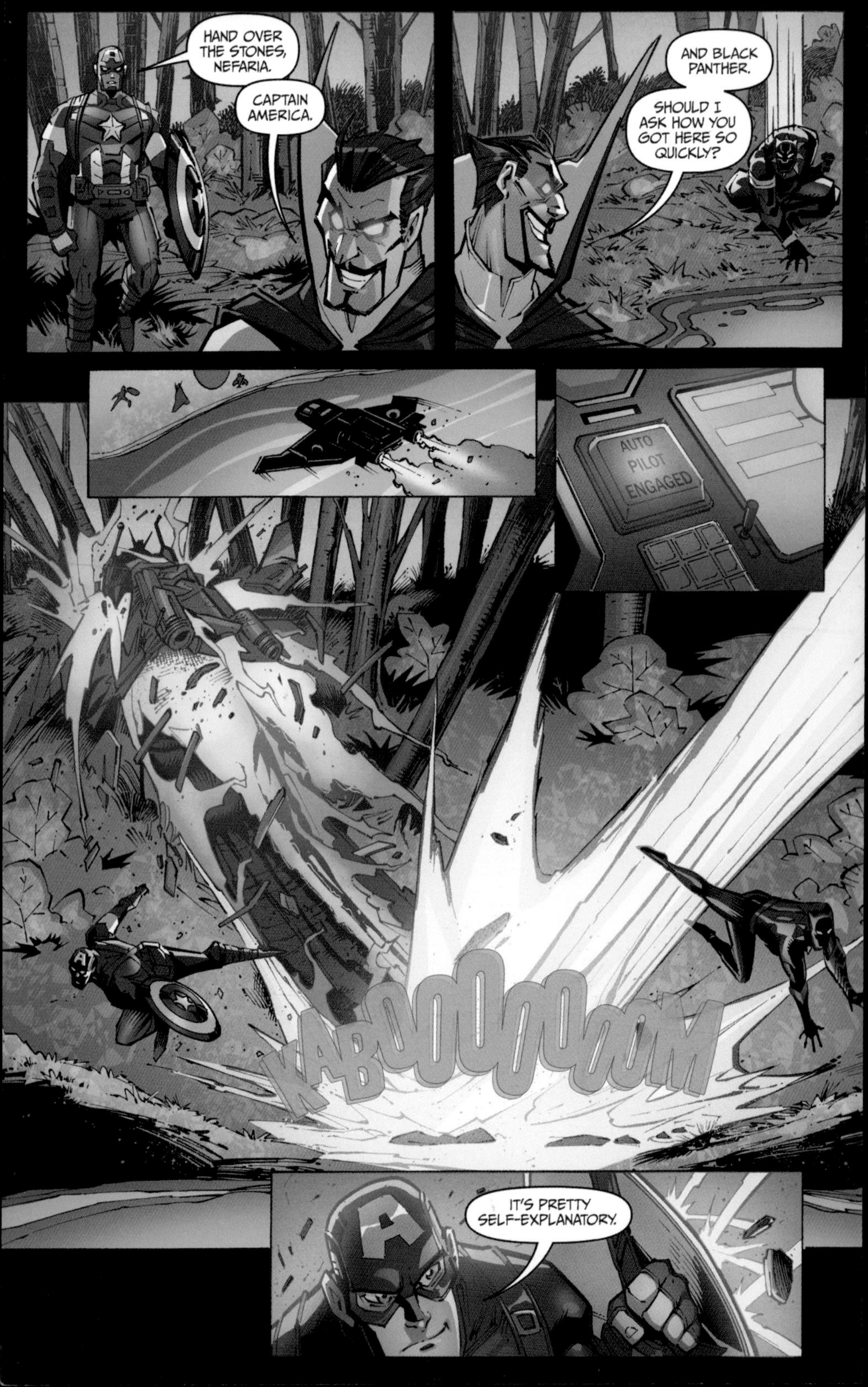
HAND OVER THE STONES, NEFARIA.
CAPTAIN AMERICA.
AND BLACK PANTHER.
SHOULD I ASK HOW YOU GOT HERE SO QUICKLY?
AUTO PILOT ENGAGED
KABOOOOOOOOM
IT'S PRETTY SELF-EXPLANATORY.

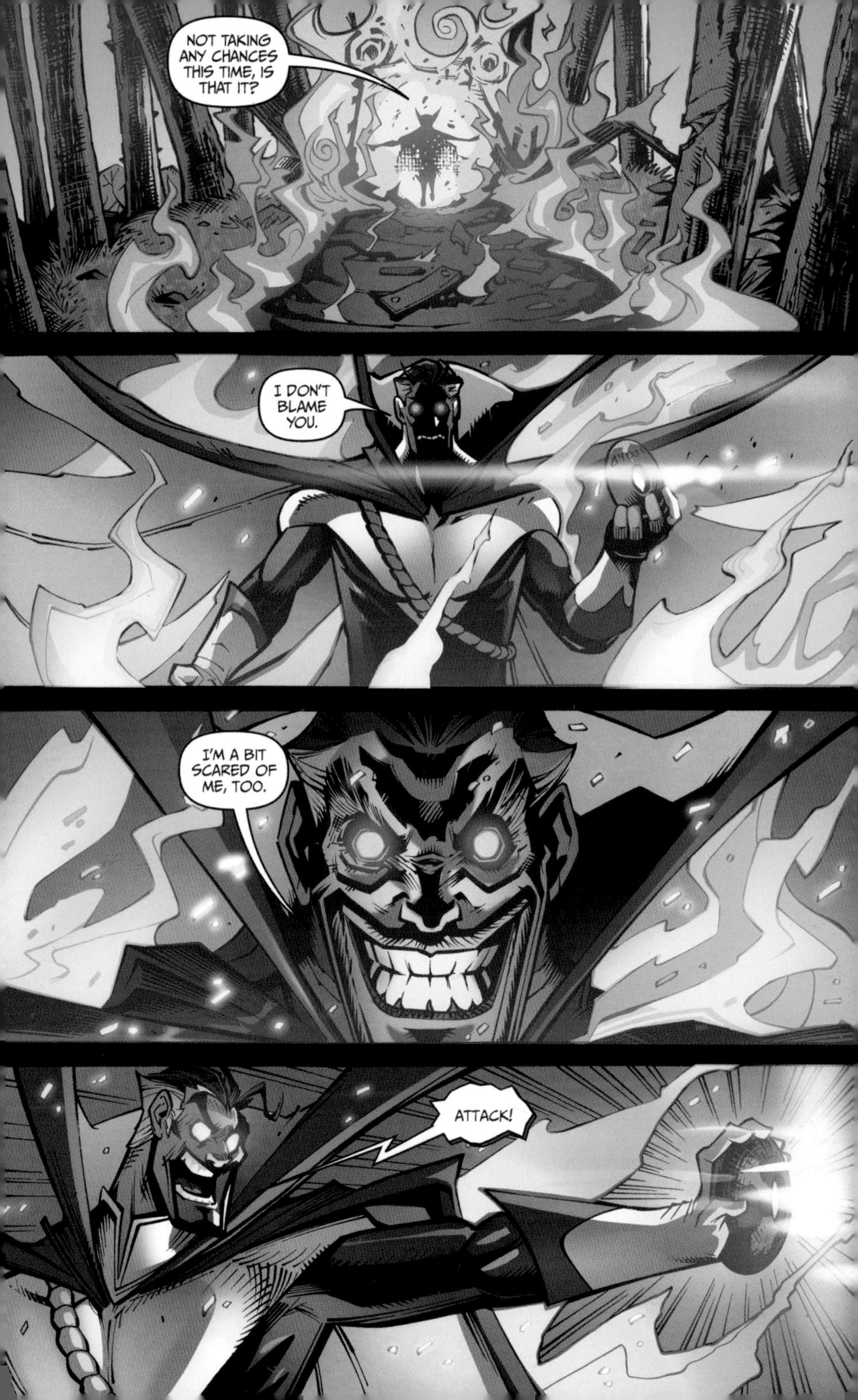
NOT TAKING ANY CHANCES THIS TIME, IS THAT IT?
I DON'T BLAME YOU.
I'M A BIT SCARED OF ME, TOO.
ATTACK!

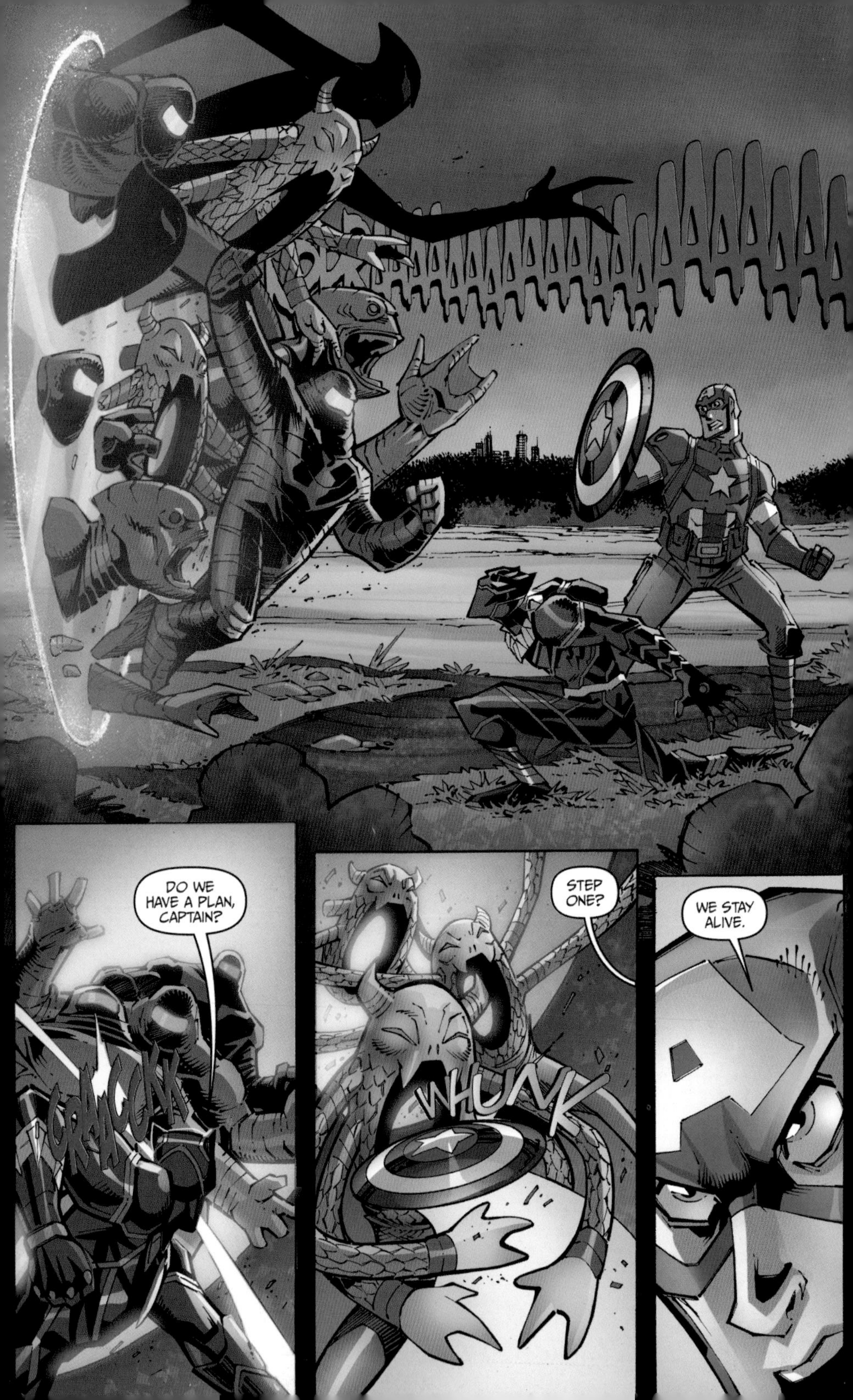

DO WE HAVE A PLAN, CAPTAIN?
CRAACK
STEP ONE?
WHUNK
WE STAY ALIVE.

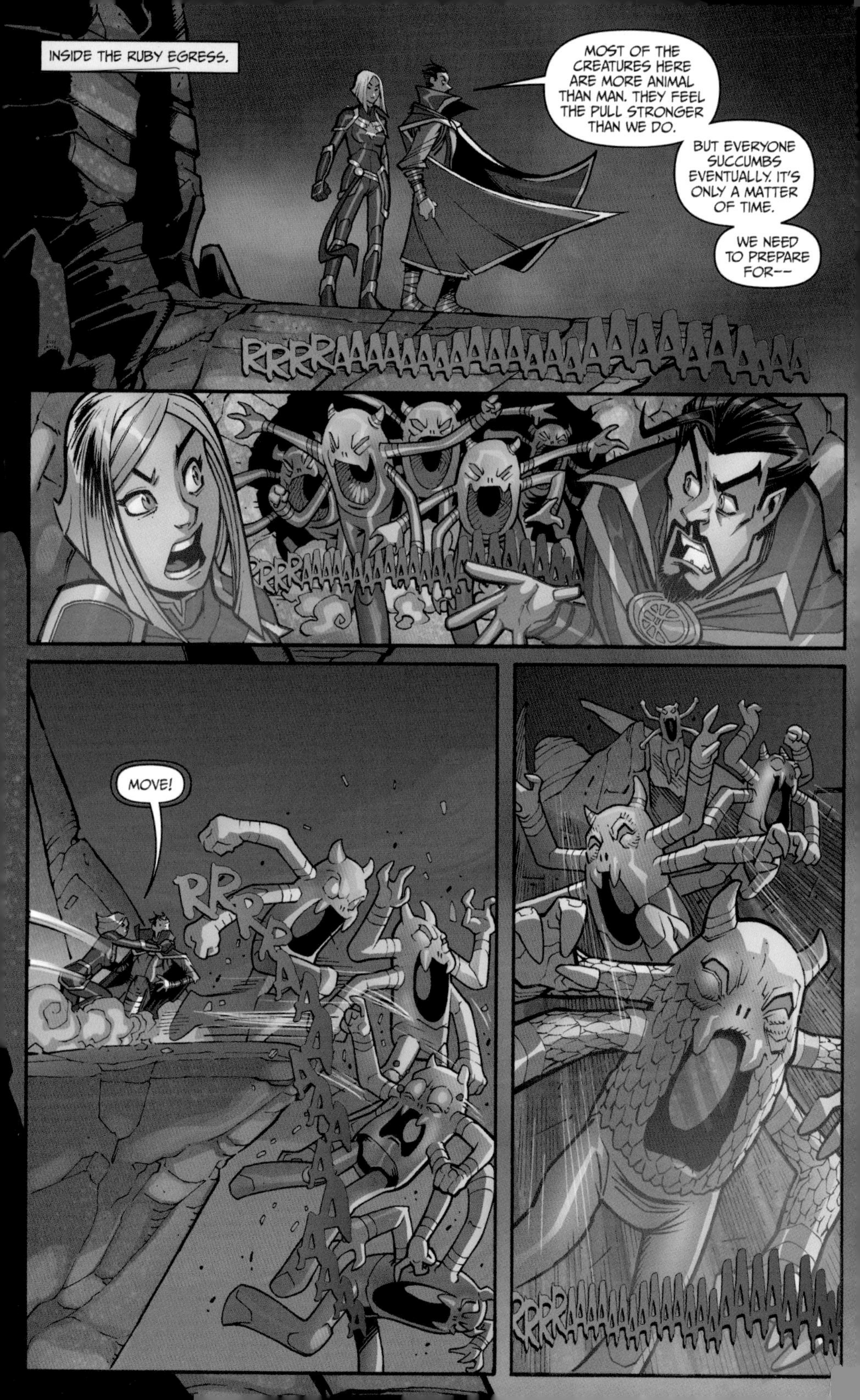
INSIDE THE RUBY EGRESS.
MOST OF THE CREATURES HERE ARE MORE ANIMAL THAN MAN. THEY FEEL THE PULL STRONGER THAN WE DO.
BUT EVERYONE SUCCUMBS EVENTUALLY. IT'S ONLY A MATTER OF TIME.
WE NEED TO PREPARE FOR--
RRRRAAAAAAAAAAAAAAAAAAAAAAAAAAAAA
RRRRAAAAAAAAAAAAAAAAAAAA
MOVE!
RRRRAAAAAAAAAAAAAA
RRRRAAAAAAAAAAAAAAAAAAAAAAAAA

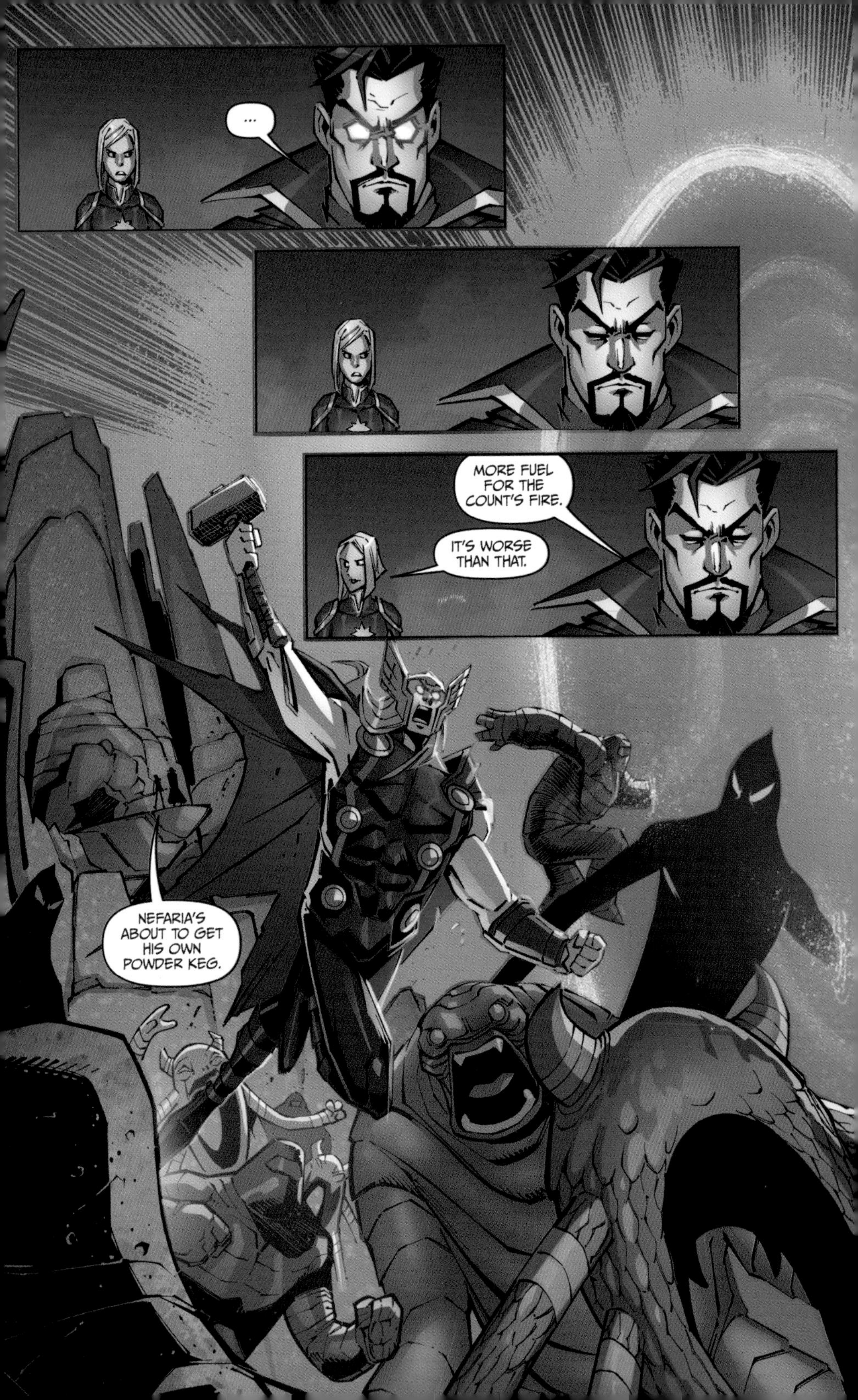
...
MORE FUEL FOR THE COUNT'S FIRE.
IT'S WORSE THAN THAT.
NEFARIA'S ABOUT TO GET HIS OWN POWDER KEG.

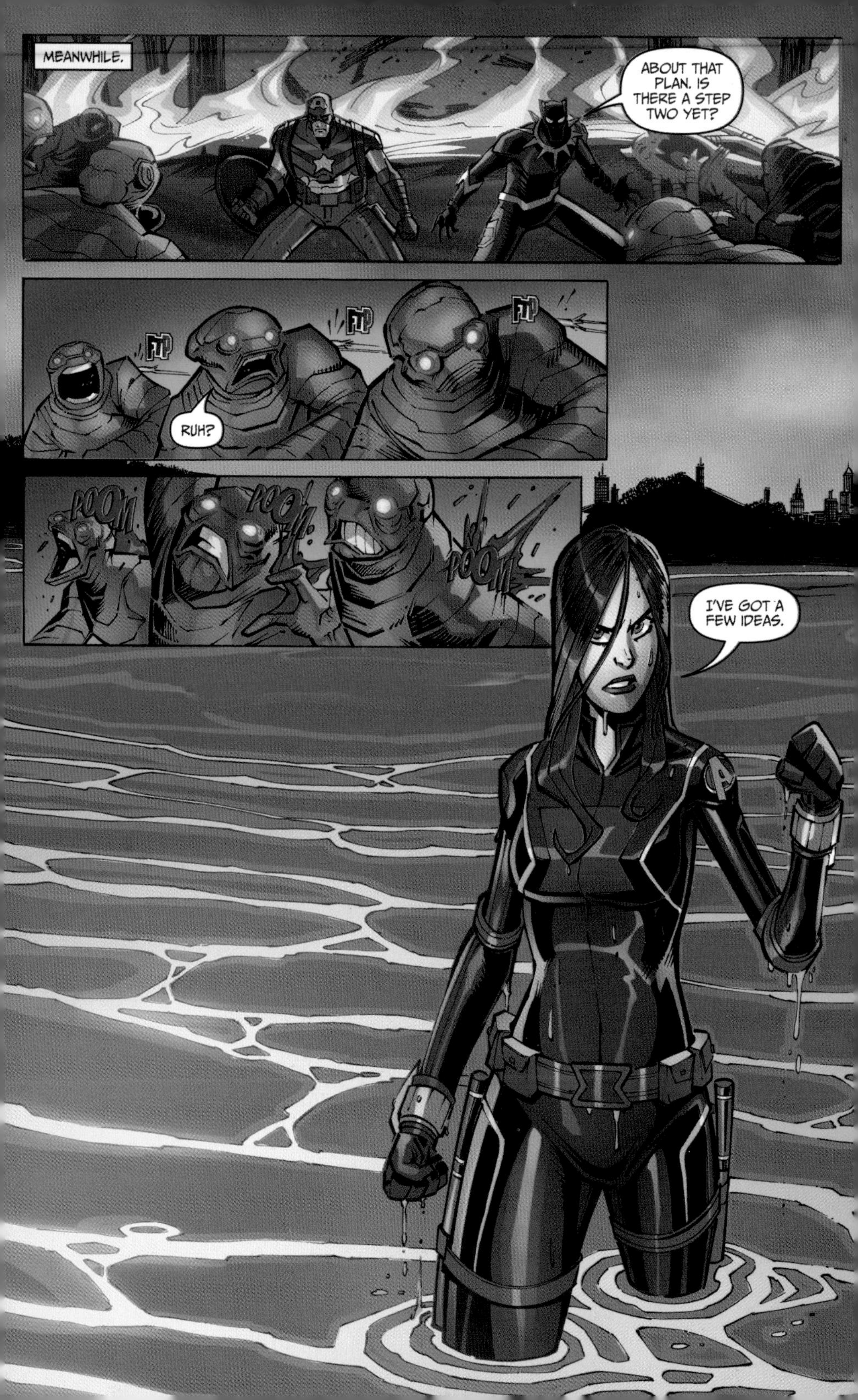

MEANWHILE.
ABOUT THAT PLAN. IS THERE A STEP TWO YET?
FTP
FTP
FTP
RUH?
POOM
POOM
POOM
I'VE GOT A FEW IDEAS.

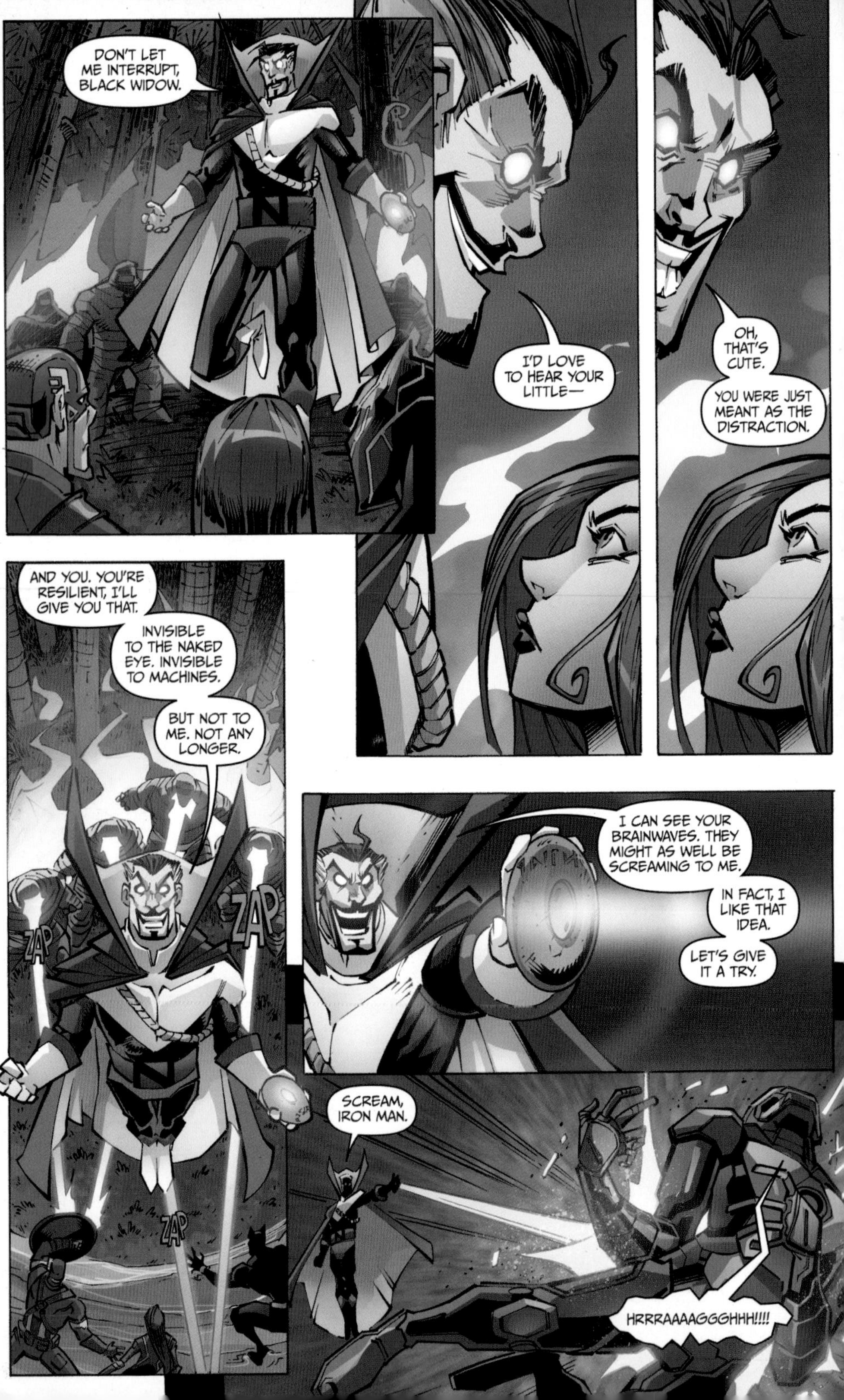

DON'T LET ME INTERRUPT, BLACK WIDOW.
I'D LOVE TO HEAR YOUR LITTLE—
OH, THAT'S CUTE.
YOU WERE JUST MEANT AS THE DISTRACTION.
AND YOU. YOU'RE RESILIENT, I'LL GIVE YOU THAT.
INVISIBLE TO THE NAKED EYE. INVISIBLE TO MACHINES.
BUT NOT TO ME. NOT ANY LONGER.
ZAP
ZAP
ZAP
I CAN SEE YOUR BRAINWAVES. THEY MIGHT AS WELL BE SCREAMING TO ME.
IN FACT, I LIKE THAT IDEA.
LET'S GIVE IT A TRY.
SCREAM, IRON MAN.
HRRRAAAAGGGHHH!!!!

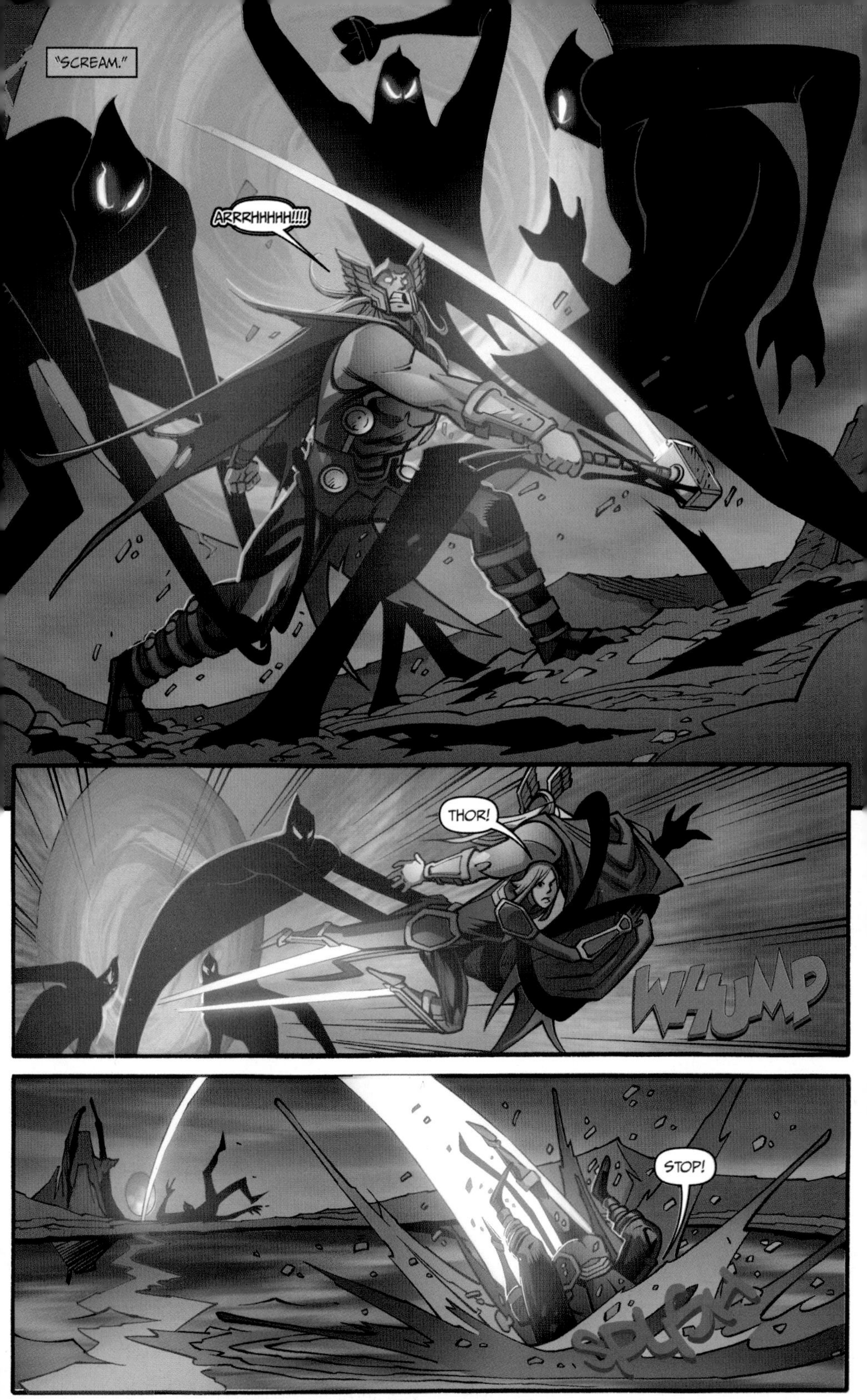
"SCREAM."
ARRRHHHHH!!!!
THOR!
WHUMP
STOP!

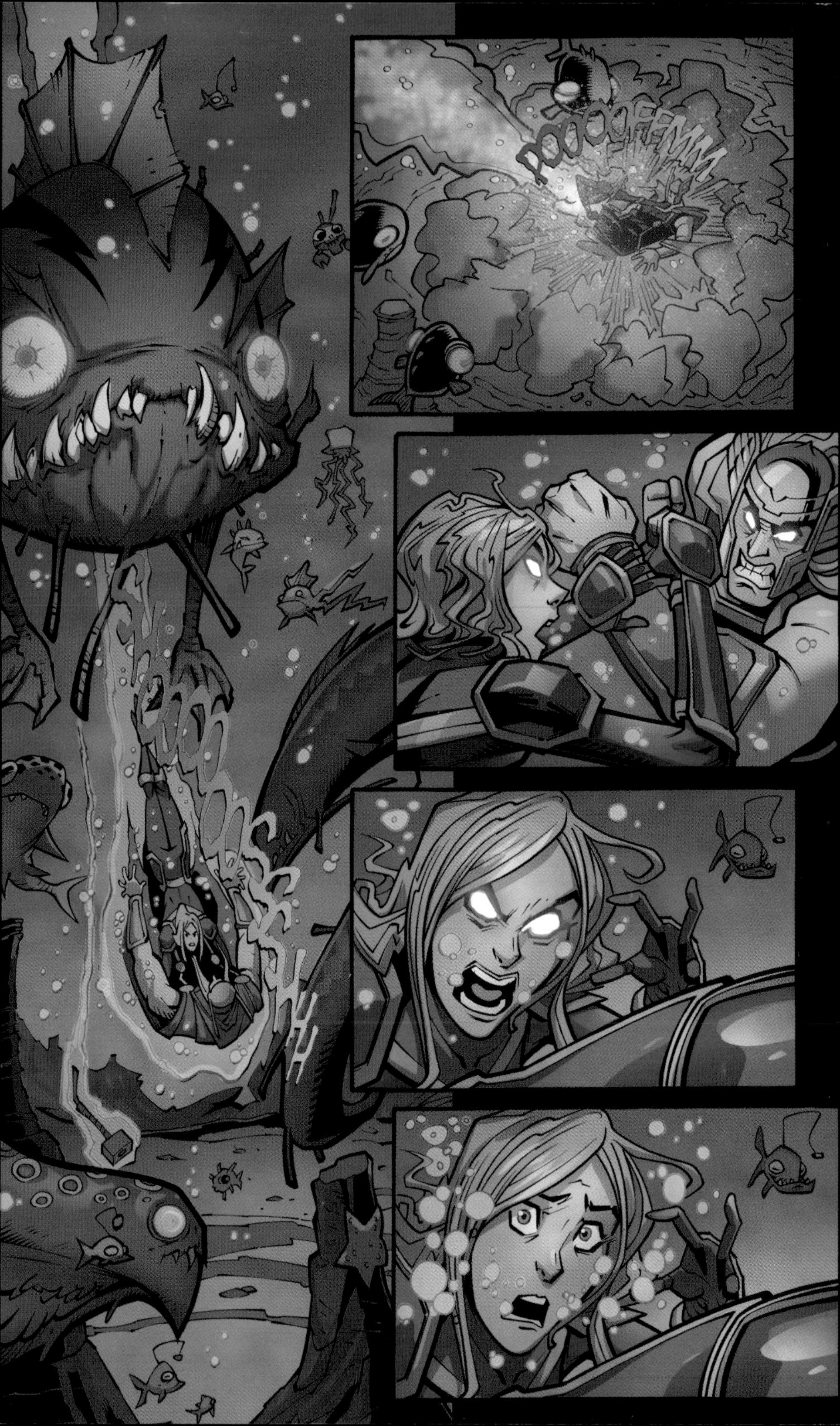
POOOOFFMMM

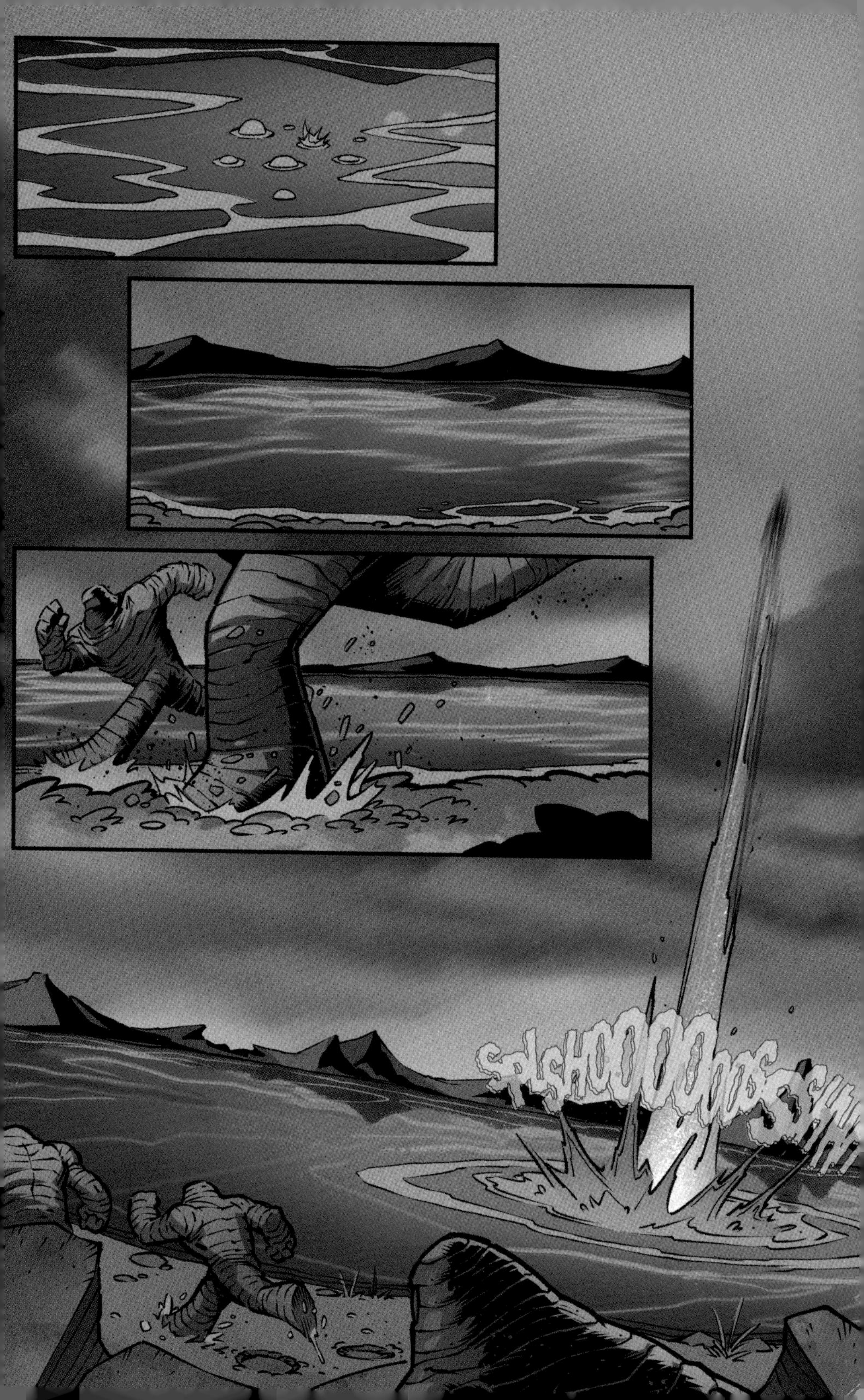
SPLSHOOOOOOSSHH

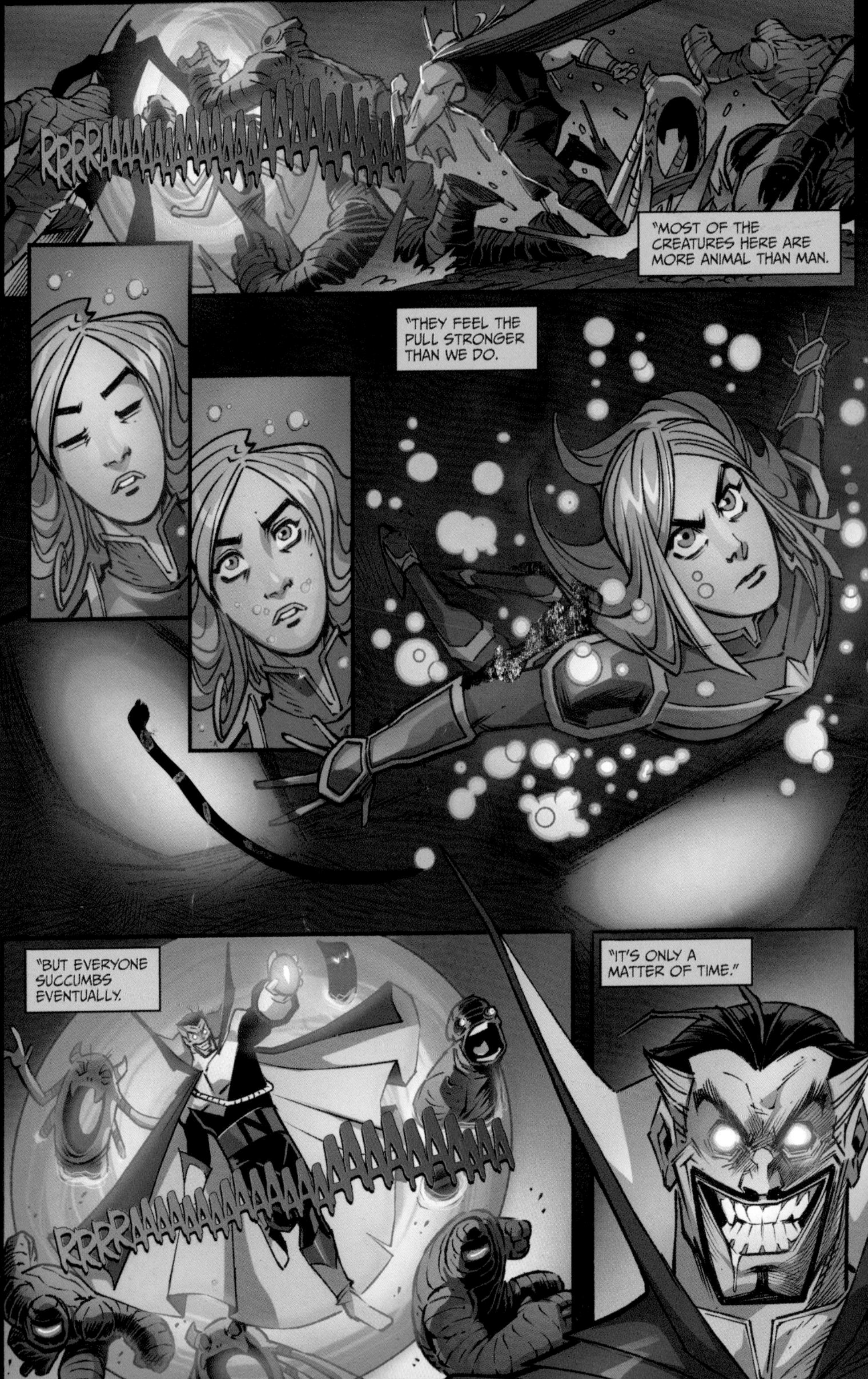
RRRRAAAAAAAAAAAAAAAAAAAAAAAA
"MOST OF THE CREATURES HERE ARE MORE ANIMAL THAN MAN.
"THEY FEEL THE PULL STRONGER THAN WE DO.
"BUT EVERYONE SUCCUMBS EVENTUALLY.
RRRRAAAAAAAAAAAAAAAAAAAAAAAAAA
"IT'S ONLY A MATTER OF TIME."

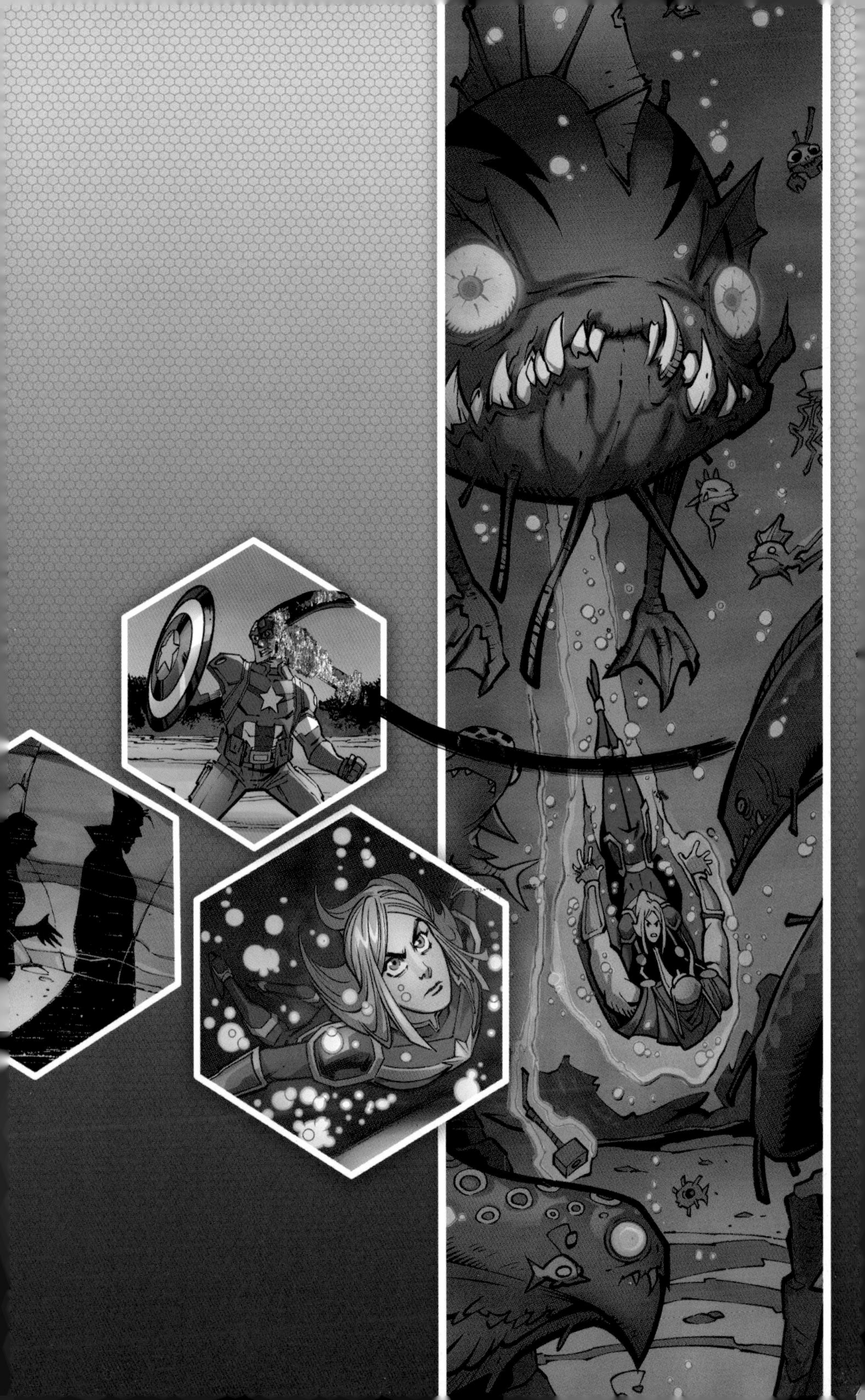

ART BY: JON SOMMARIVA

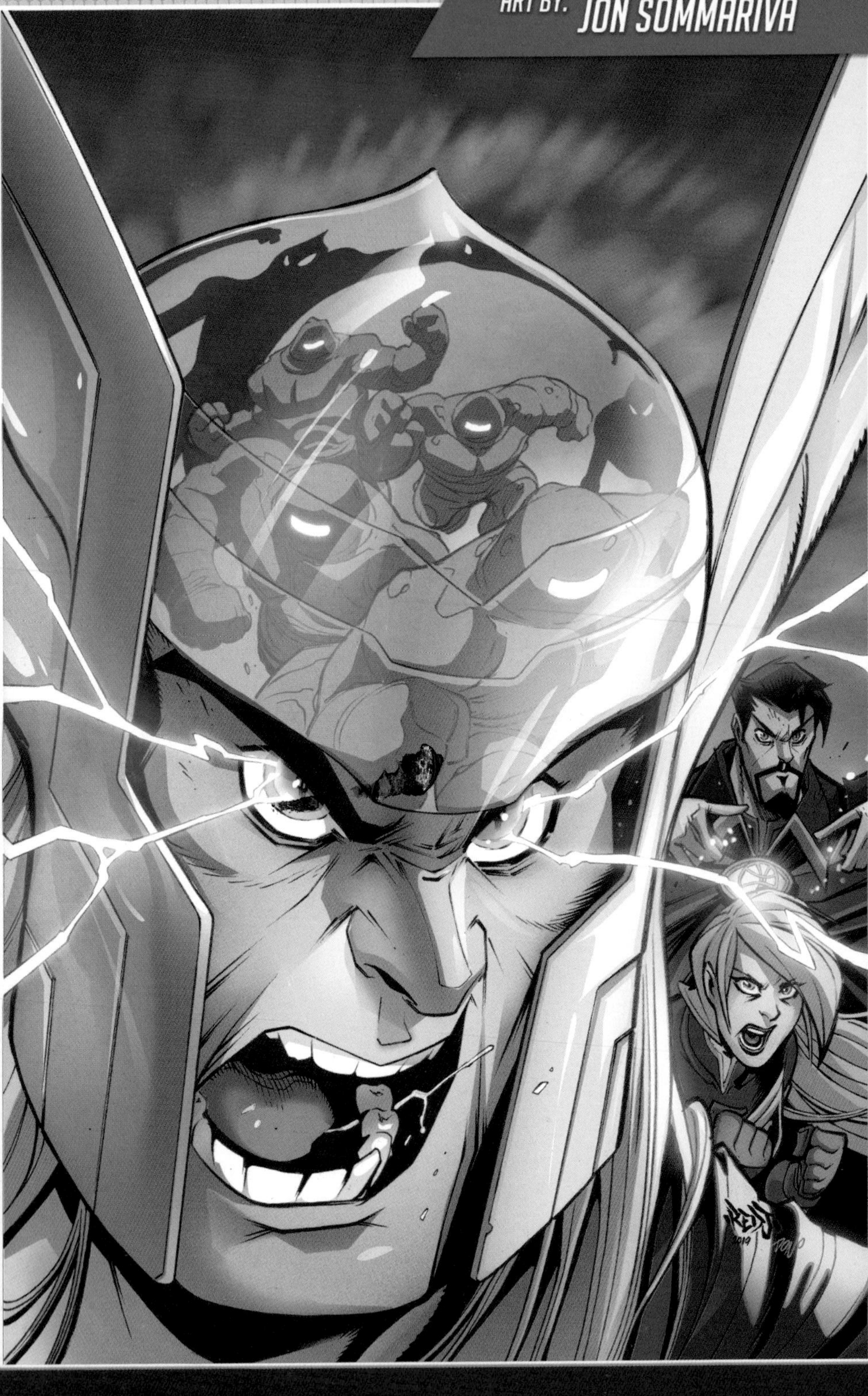

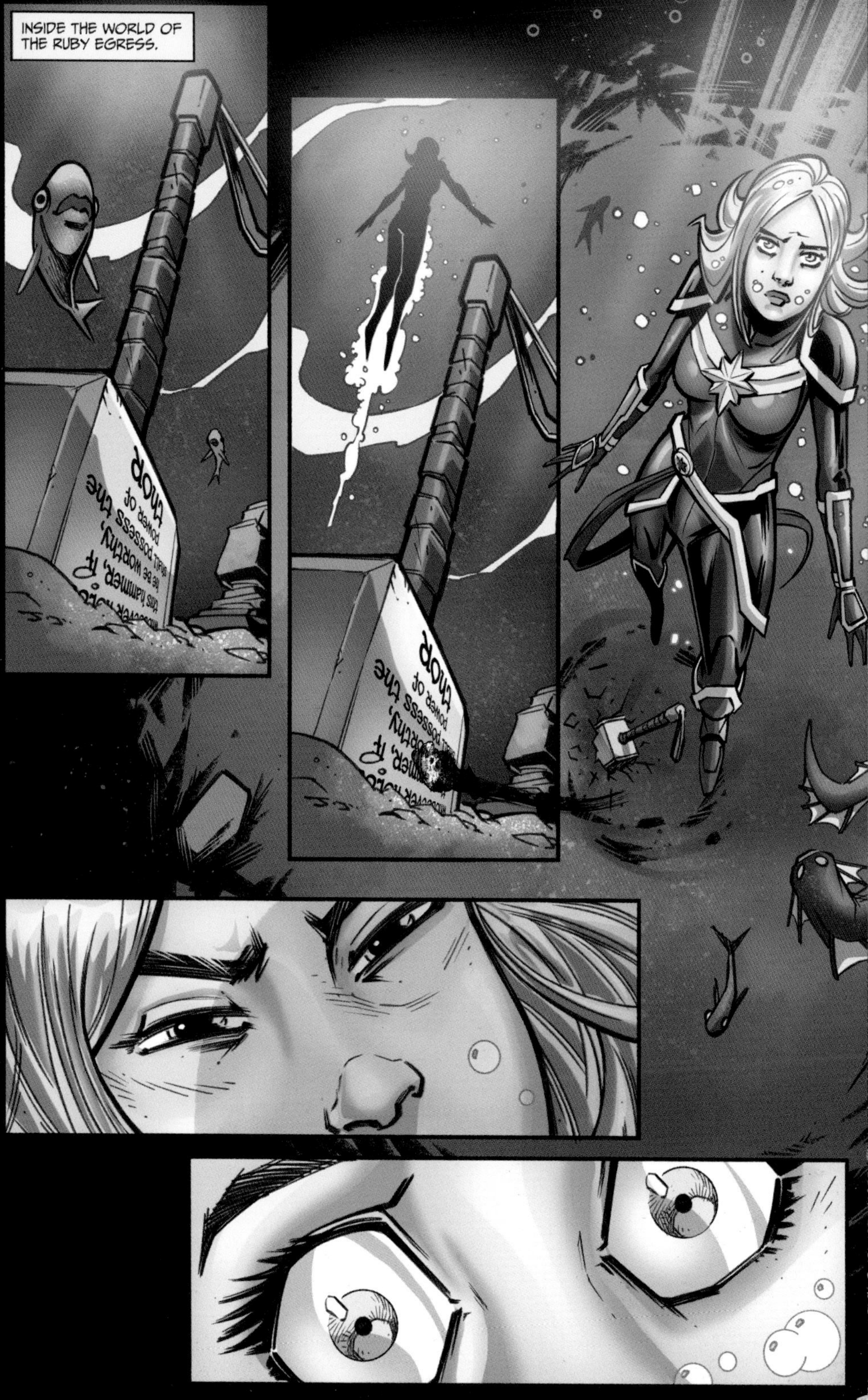
INSIDE THE WORLD OF THE RUBY EGRESS.

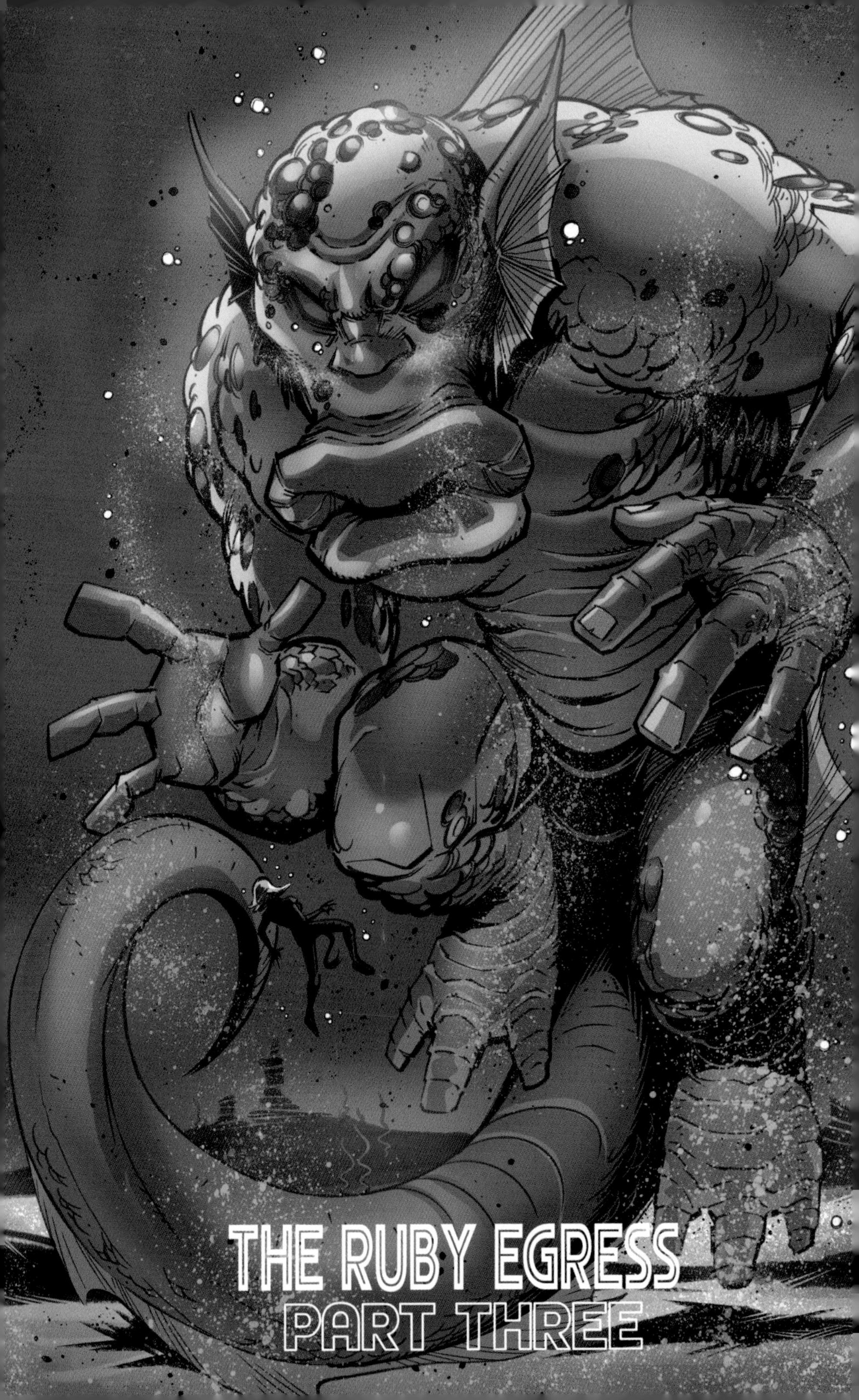
THE RUBY EGRESS
PART THREE

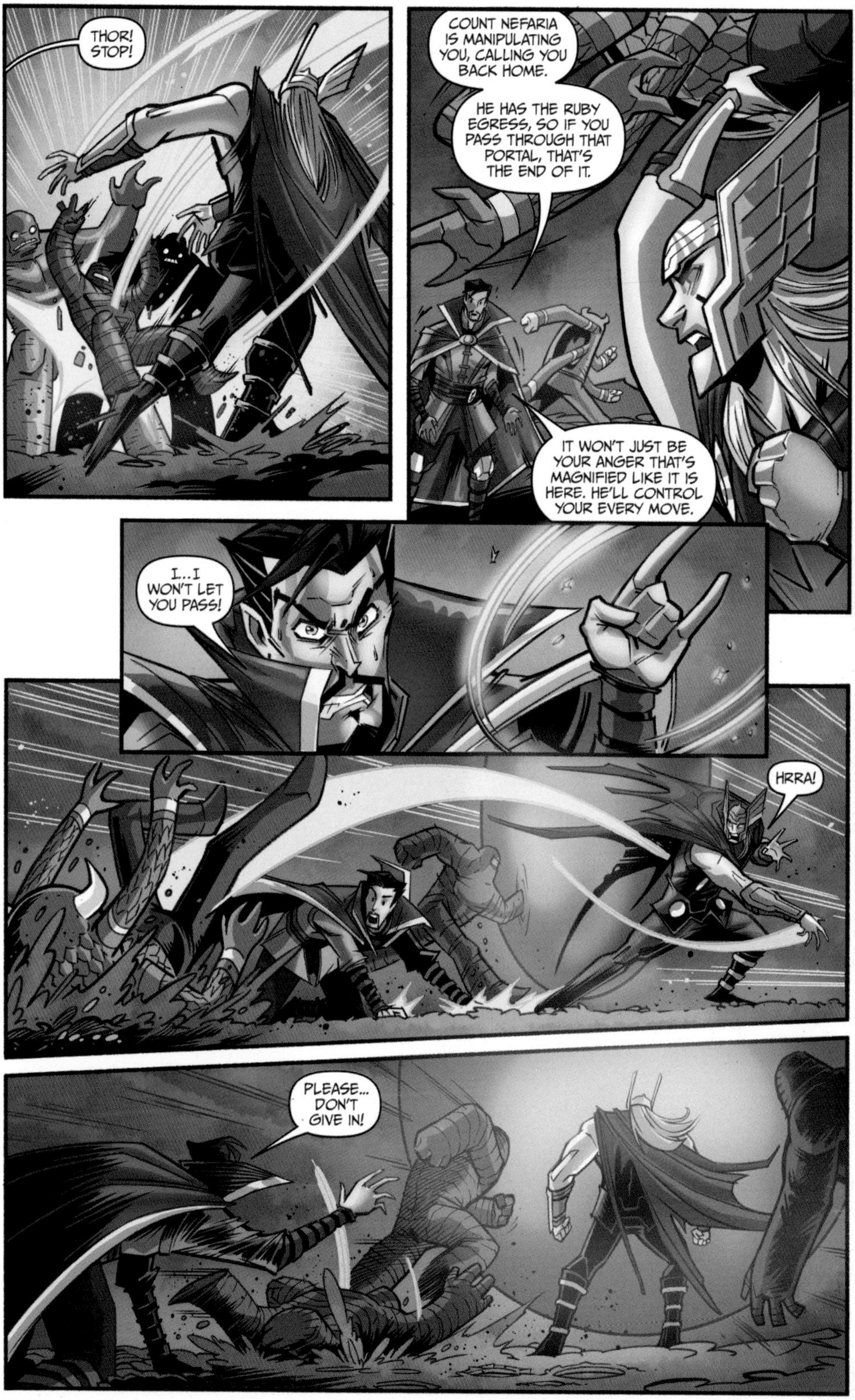
THOR! STOP!
COUNT NEFARIA IS MANIPULATING YOU, CALLING YOU BACK HOME.
HE HAS THE RUBY EGRESS, SO IF YOU PASS THROUGH THAT PORTAL, THAT'S THE END OF IT.
IT WON'T JUST BE YOUR ANGER THAT'S MAGNIFIED LIKE IT IS HERE. HE'LL CONTROL YOUR EVERY MOVE.
I...I WON'T LET YOU PASS!
HRRA!
PLEASE... DON'T GIVE IN!

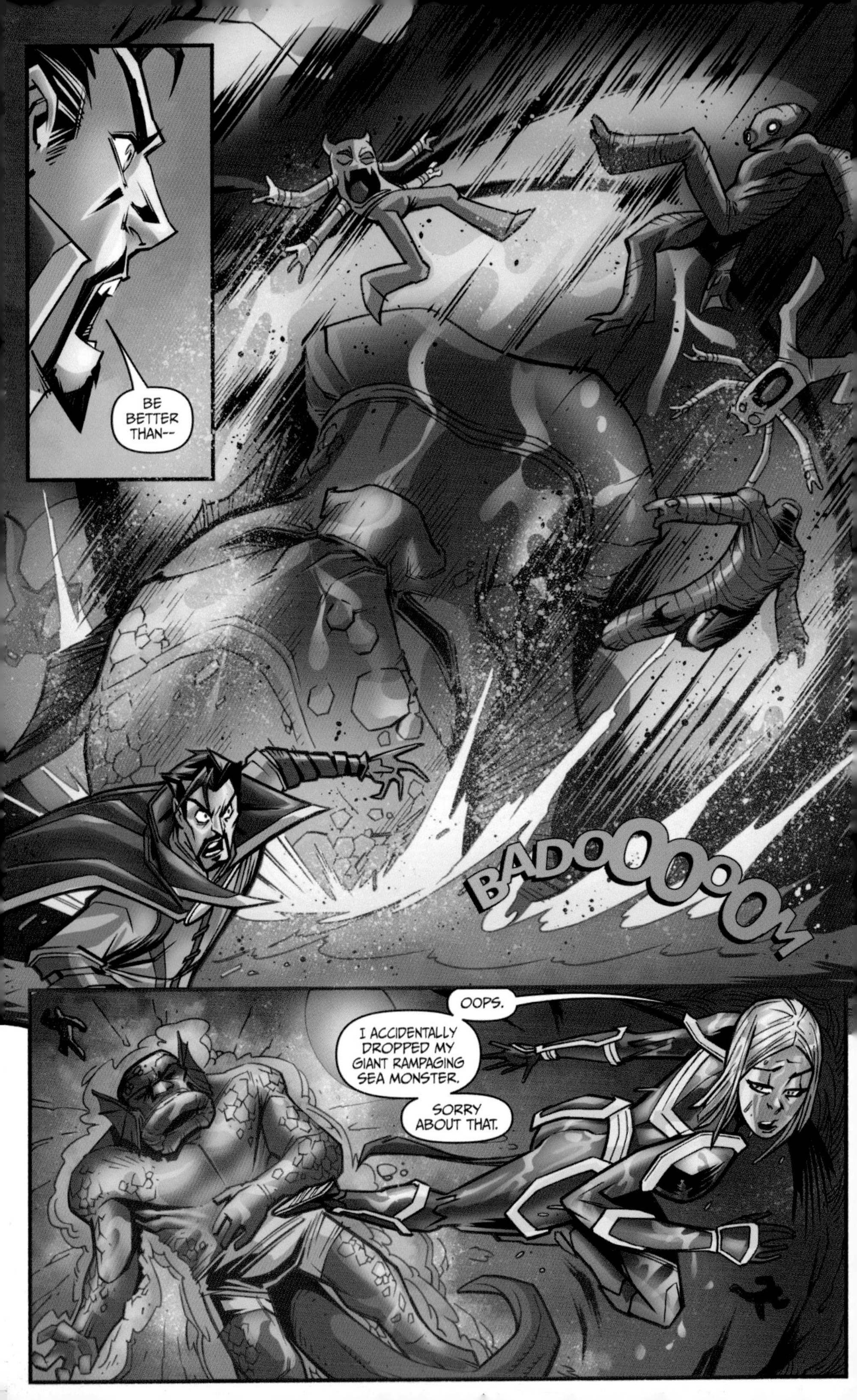
BE BETTER THAN--
BADOOOO-OOM
OOPS.
I ACCIDENTALLY DROPPED MY GIANT RAMPAGING SEA MONSTER.
SORRY ABOUT THAT.

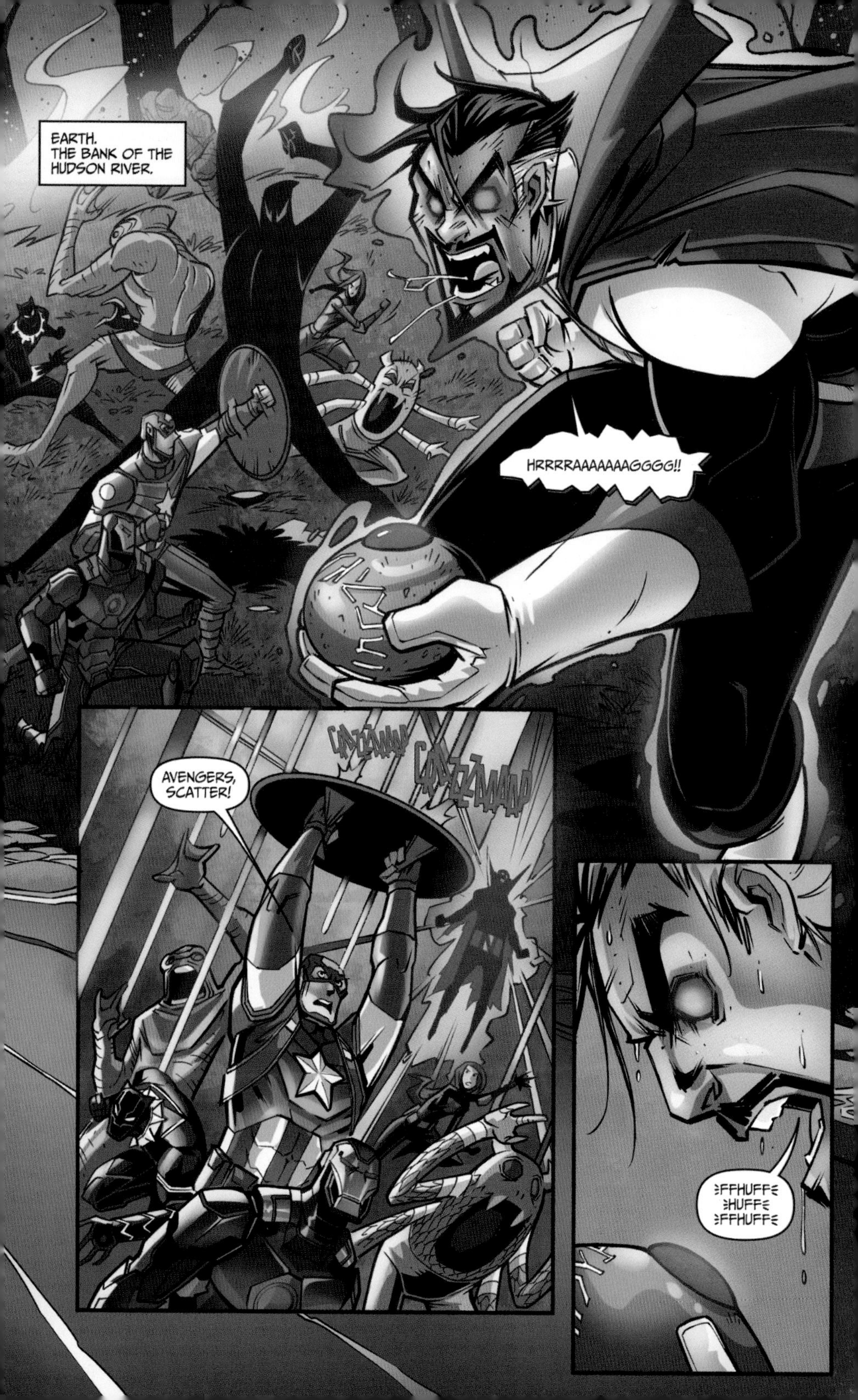
EARTH.
THE BANK OF THE
HUDSON RIVER.
HRRRRAAAAAAAAGGGG!!
AVENGERS,
SCATTER!
FFHUFF
HUFF
FFHUFF

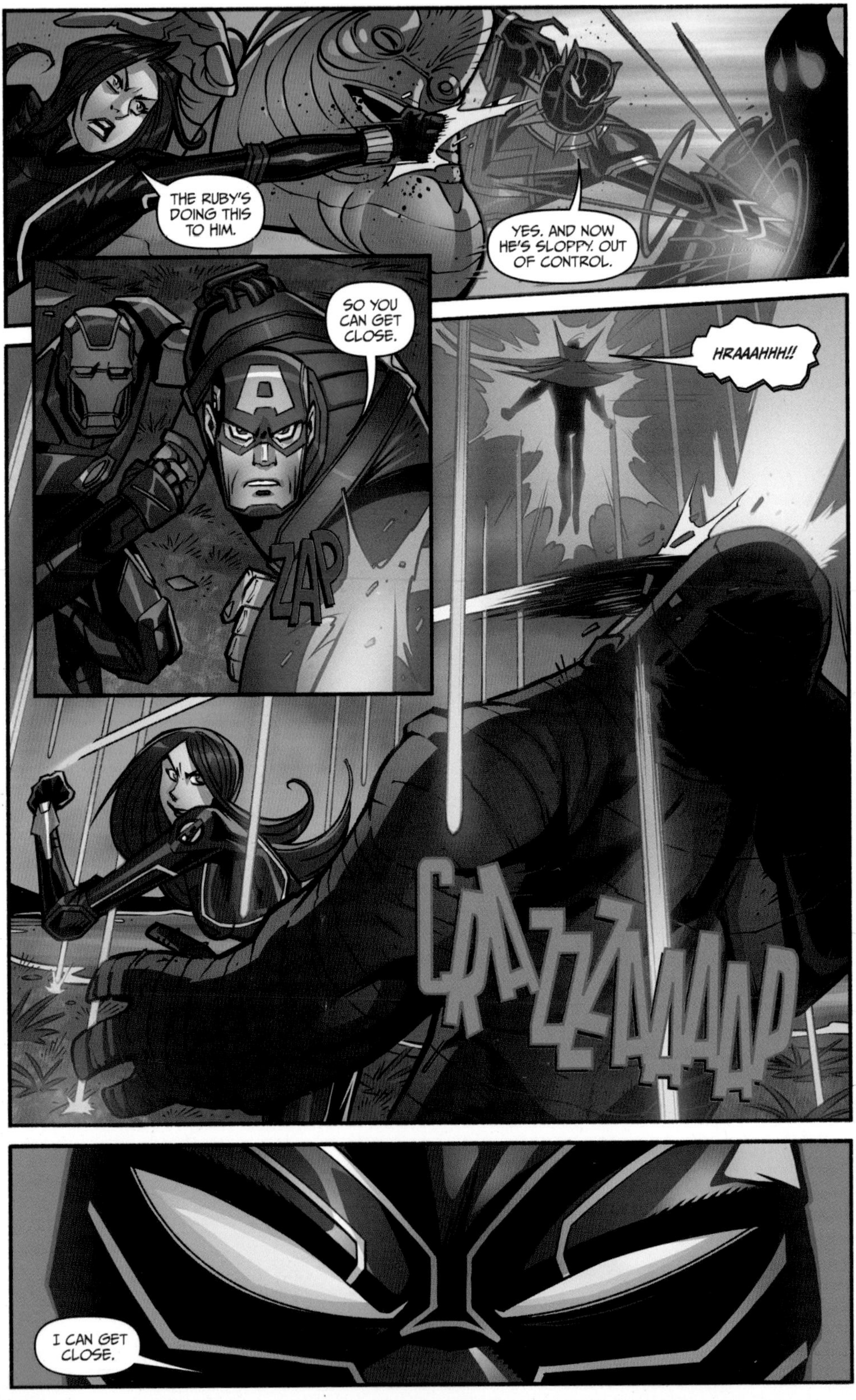
THE RUBY'S DOING THIS TO HIM.
YES. AND NOW HE'S SLOPPY. OUT OF CONTROL.
SO YOU CAN GET CLOSE.
ZAP
HRAAAHHH!!
CRAZZZAAAAP
I CAN GET CLOSE.

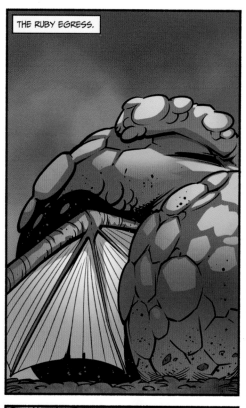

THE RUBY EGRESS.

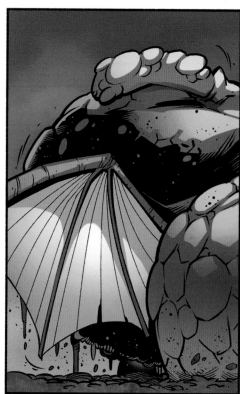

HRRRRR--

--UUPHH!

BOOM!

YOU CALM ENOUGH FOR A CONVERSATION YET?

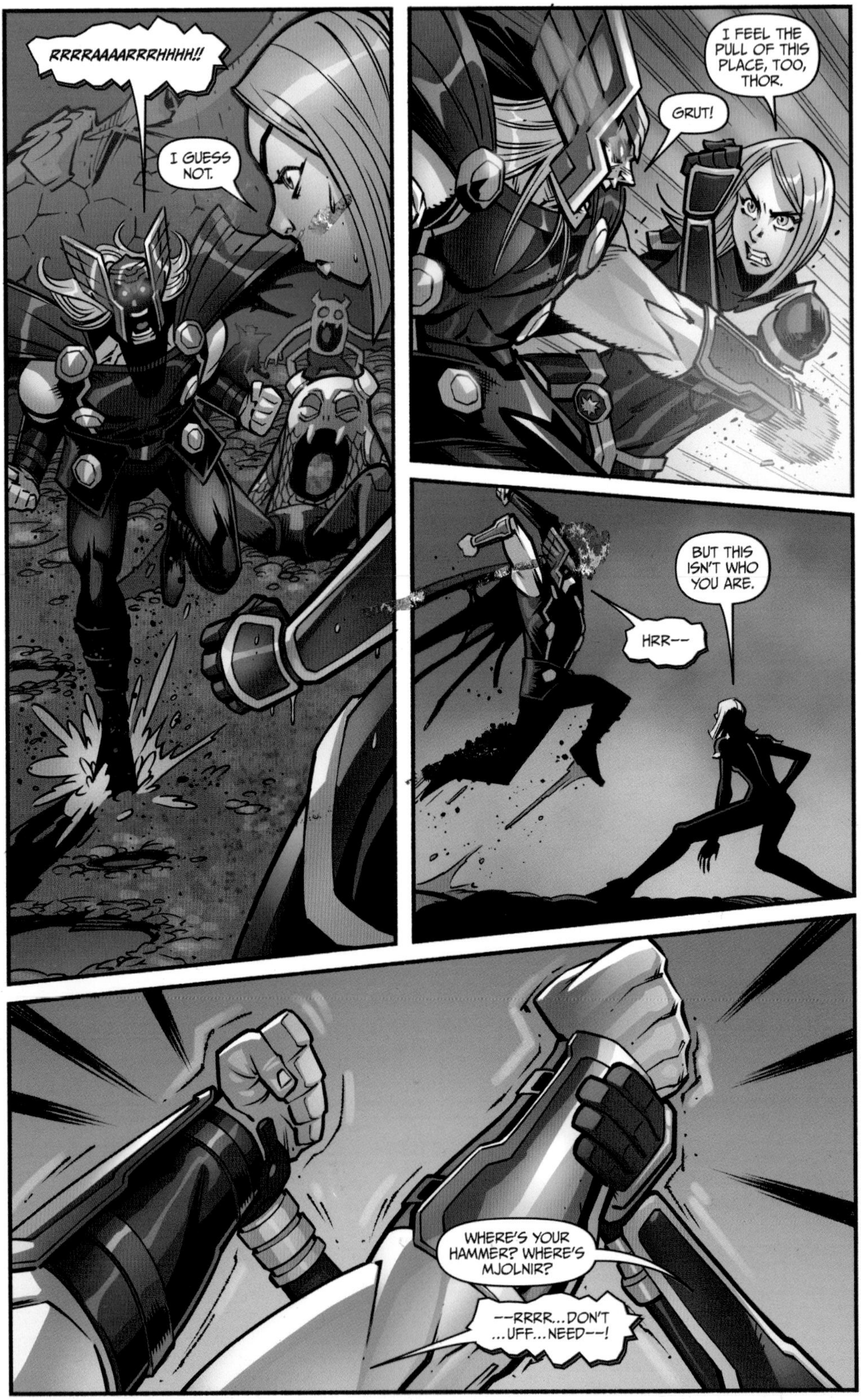

RRRRAAAARRRHHHH!!
I GUESS NOT.
I FEEL THE PULL OF THIS PLACE, TOO, THOR.
GRUT!
BUT THIS ISN'T WHO YOU ARE.
HRR--
WHERE'S YOUR HAMMER? WHERE'S MJOLNIR?
--RRRR...DON'T ...UFF...NEED--!

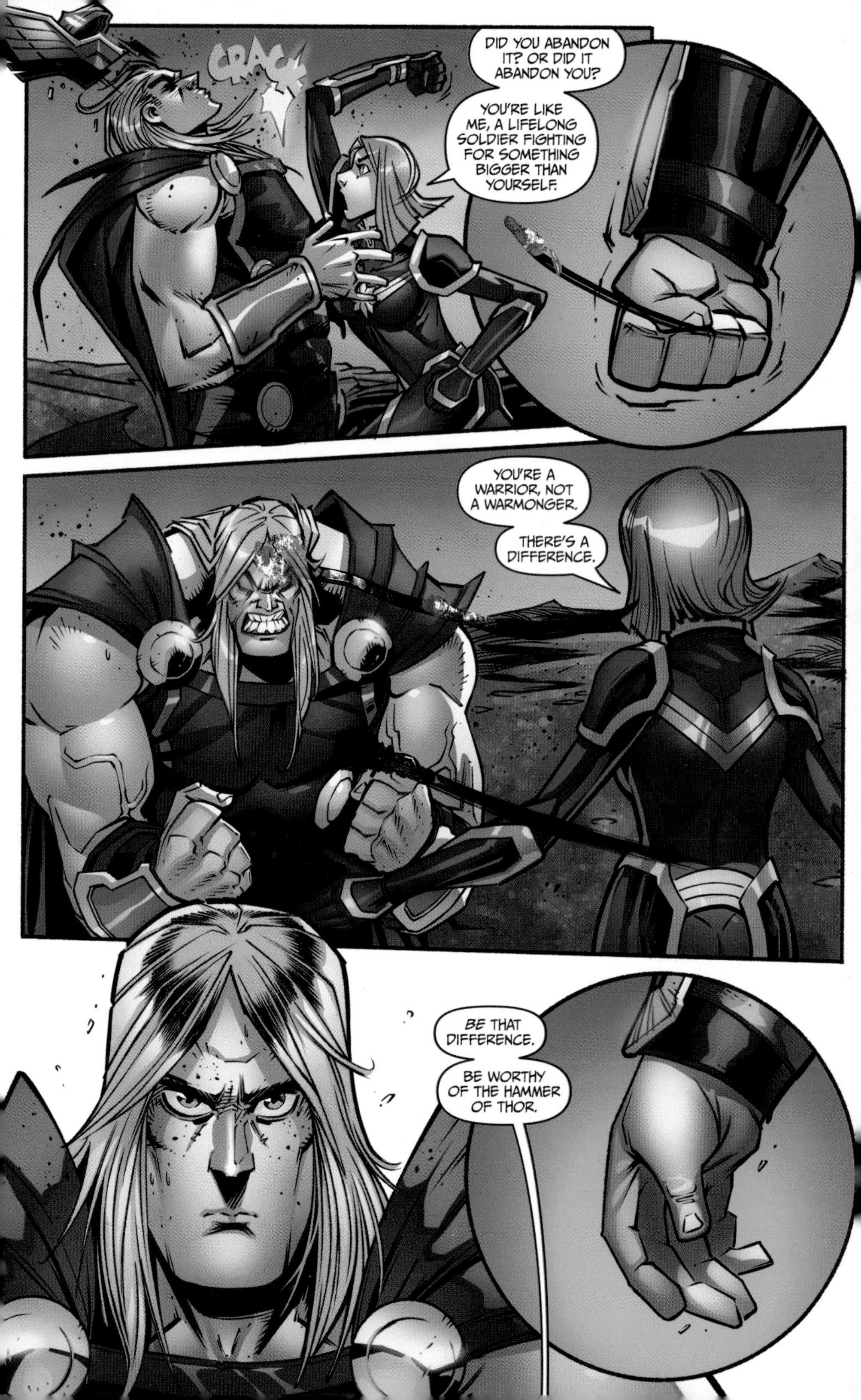
CRACK
DID YOU ABANDON IT? OR DID IT ABANDON YOU?
YOU'RE LIKE ME, A LIFELONG SOLDIER FIGHTING FOR SOMETHING BIGGER THAN YOURSELF.
YOU'RE A WARRIOR, NOT A WARMONGER.
THERE'S A DIFFERENCE.
BE THAT DIFFERENCE.
BE WORTHY OF THE HAMMER OF THOR.

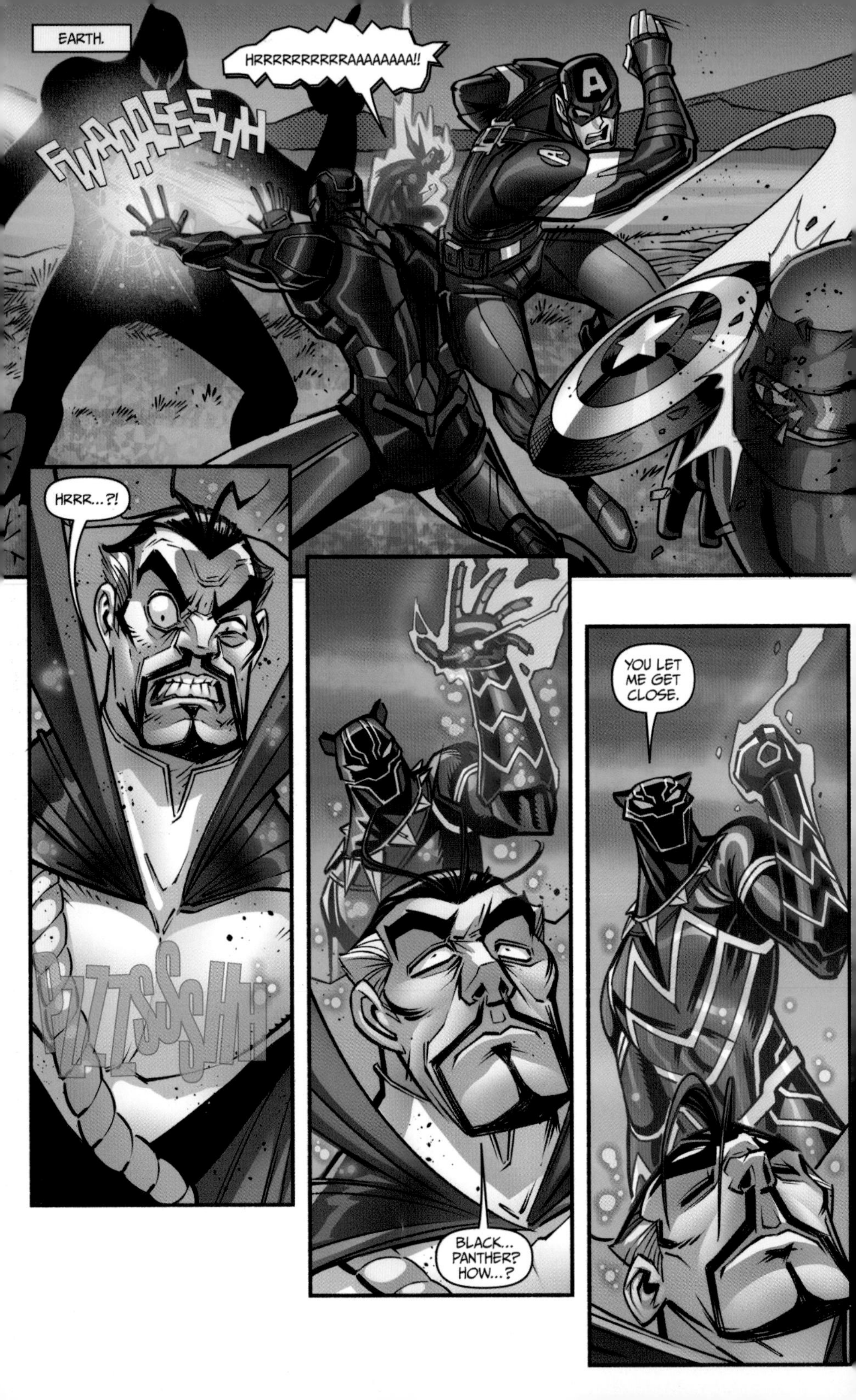
EARTH.
HRRRRRRRRRRAAAAAAAA!!
FWOOOSSSHH
HRRR...?!
BLACK... PANTHER? HOW...?
YOU LET ME GET CLOSE.

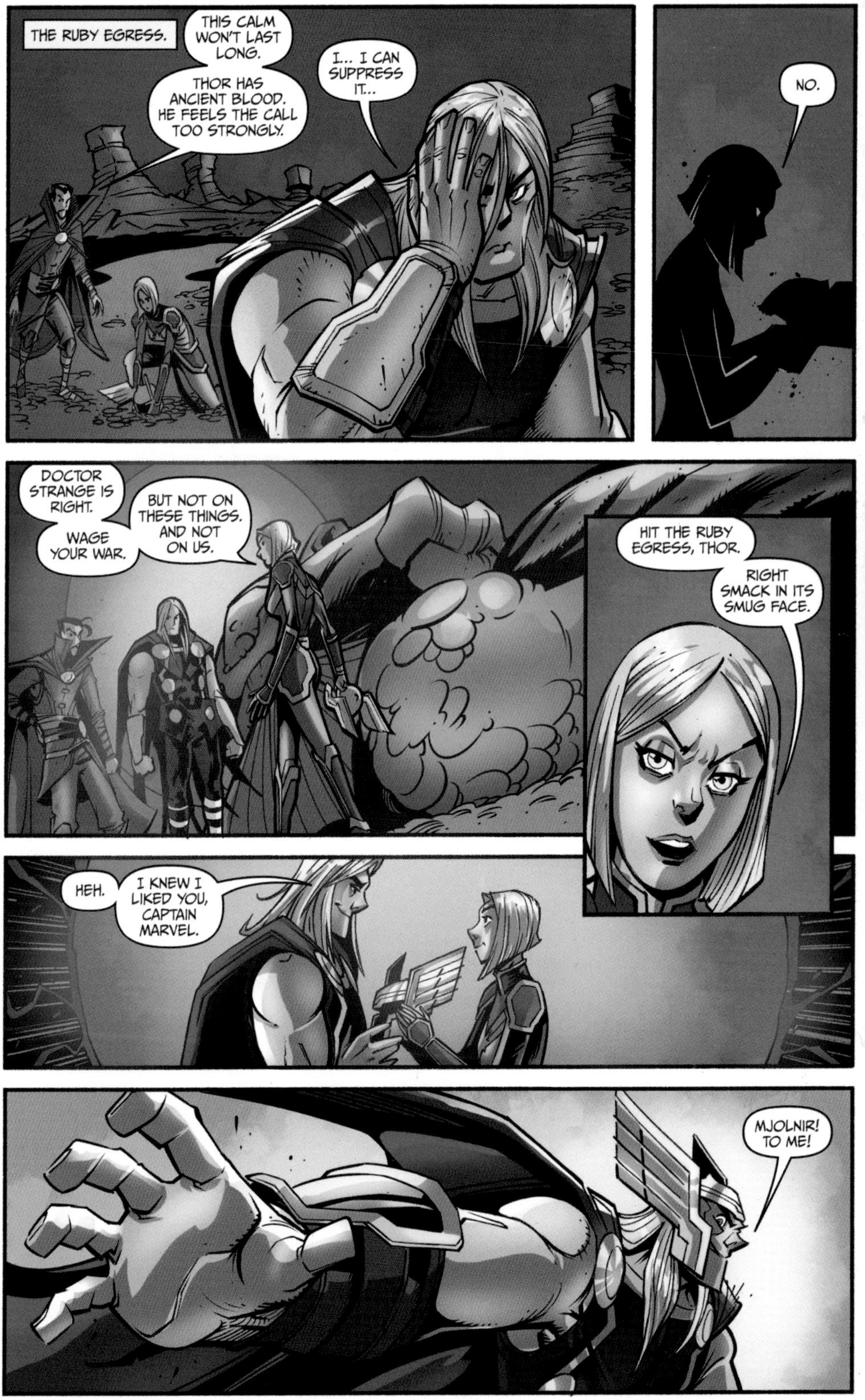
THE RUBY EGRESS.
THIS CALM WON'T LAST LONG.
THOR HAS ANCIENT BLOOD. HE FEELS THE CALL TOO STRONGLY.
I... I CAN SUPPRESS IT...
NO.
DOCTOR STRANGE IS RIGHT.
WAGE YOUR WAR.
BUT NOT ON THESE THINGS. AND NOT ON US.
HIT THE RUBY EGRESS, THOR.
RIGHT SMACK IN ITS SMUG FACE.
HEH.
I KNEW I LIKED YOU, CAPTAIN MARVEL.
MJOLNIR! TO ME!

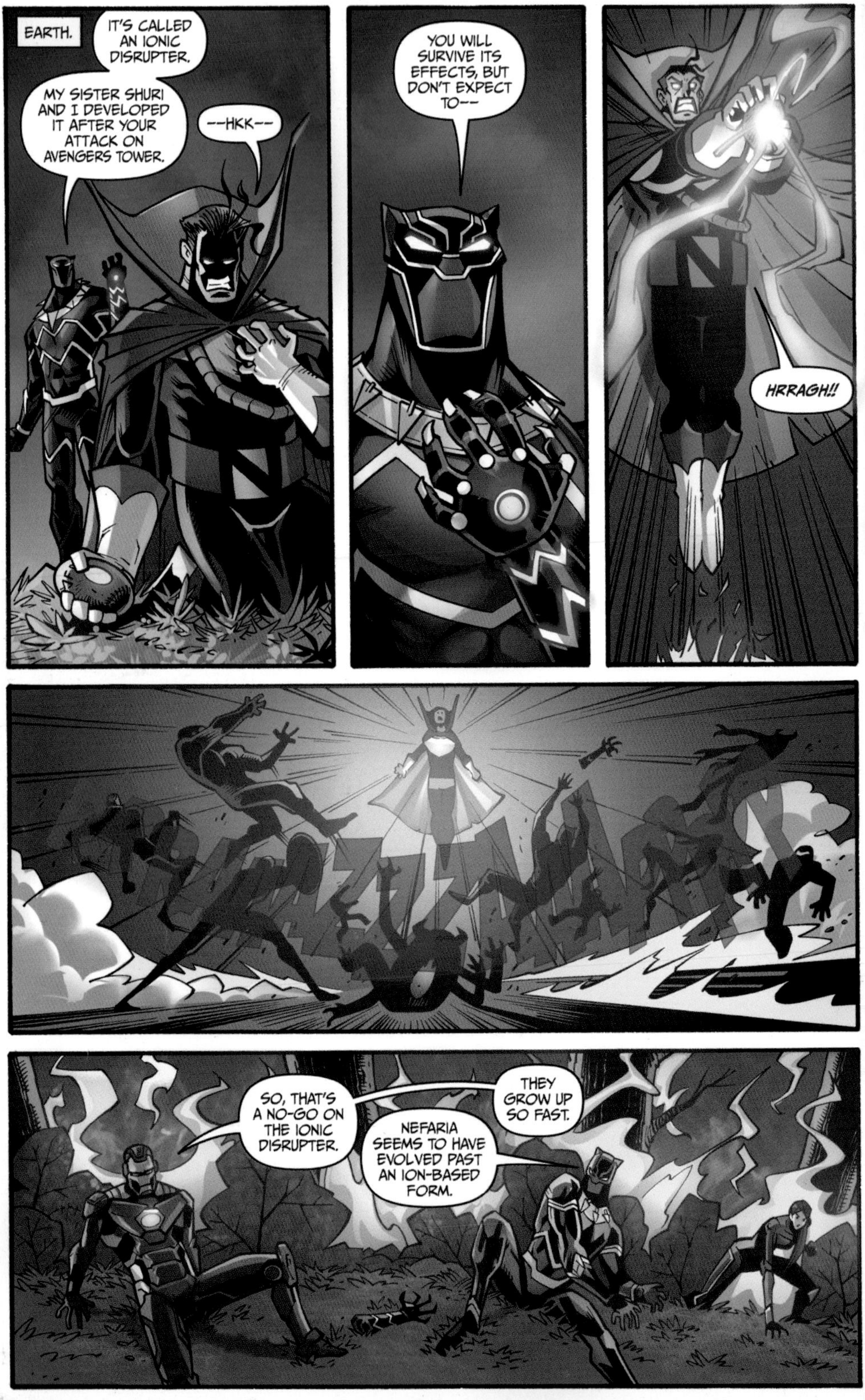
EARTH.
IT'S CALLED AN IONIC DISRUPTER.
MY SISTER SHURI AND I DEVELOPED IT AFTER YOUR ATTACK ON AVENGERS TOWER.
--HKK--
YOU WILL SURVIVE ITS EFFECTS, BUT DON'T EXPECT TO--
HRRAGH!!
SO, THAT'S A NO-GO ON THE IONIC DISRUPTER.
THEY GROW UP SO FAST.
NEFARIA SEEMS TO HAVE EVOLVED PAST AN ION-BASED FORM.

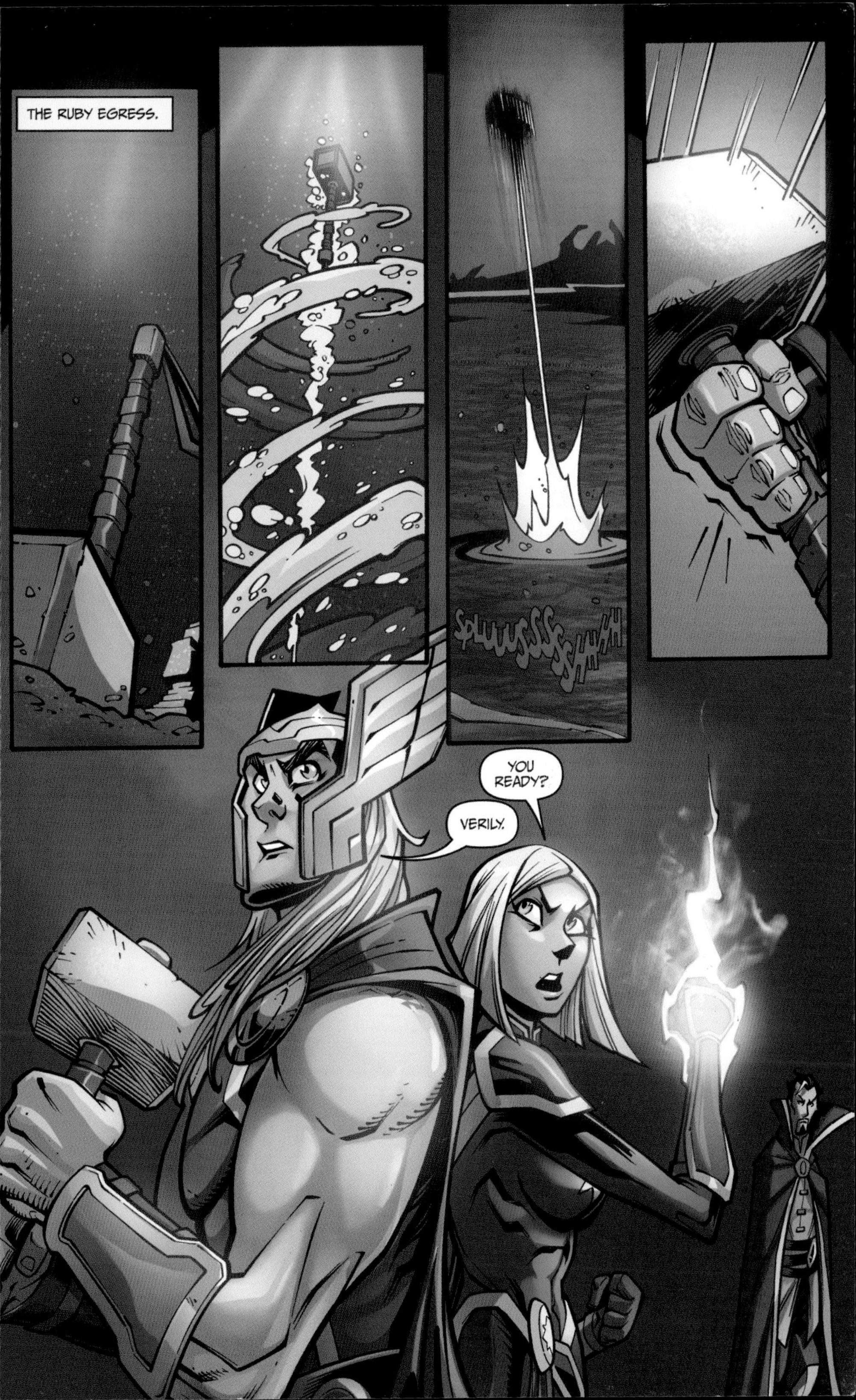
THE RUBY EGRESS.
SPLUUUSSSSSSHHHH
YOU READY?
VERILY.

THEN LET'S REDIRECT THAT ANGER, SOLDIER...

...AND SEE HOW MUCH POWER NEFARIA CAN HANDLE!

FWAAAFSH!!

FOR MIDGARD!

FOR THE AVENGERS!

KRAKKA-BOOOOM

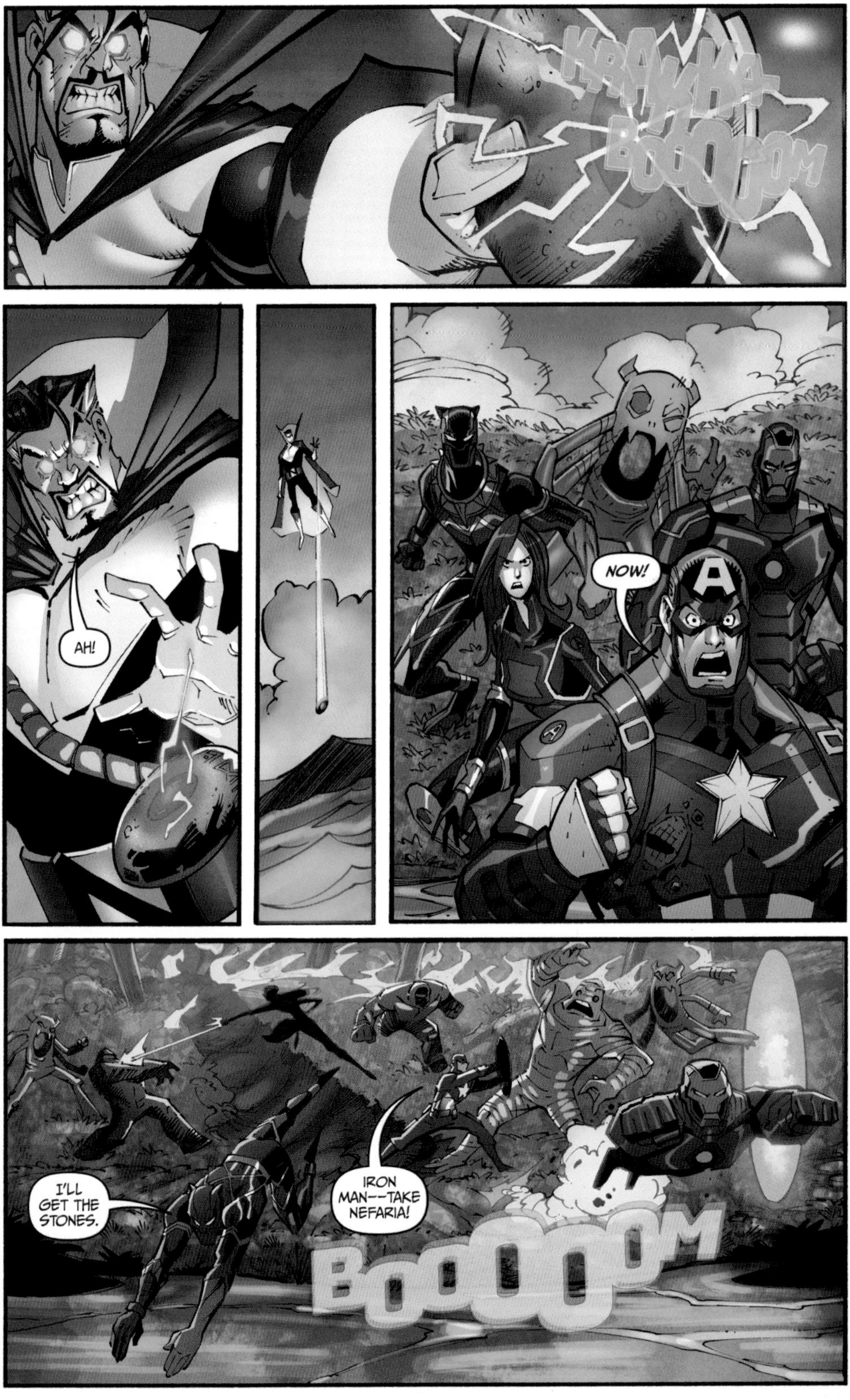
KRAKKA-BOOOOOM
AH!
NOW!
I'LL GET THE STONES.
IRON MAN--TAKE NEFARIA!
BOOOOOOM

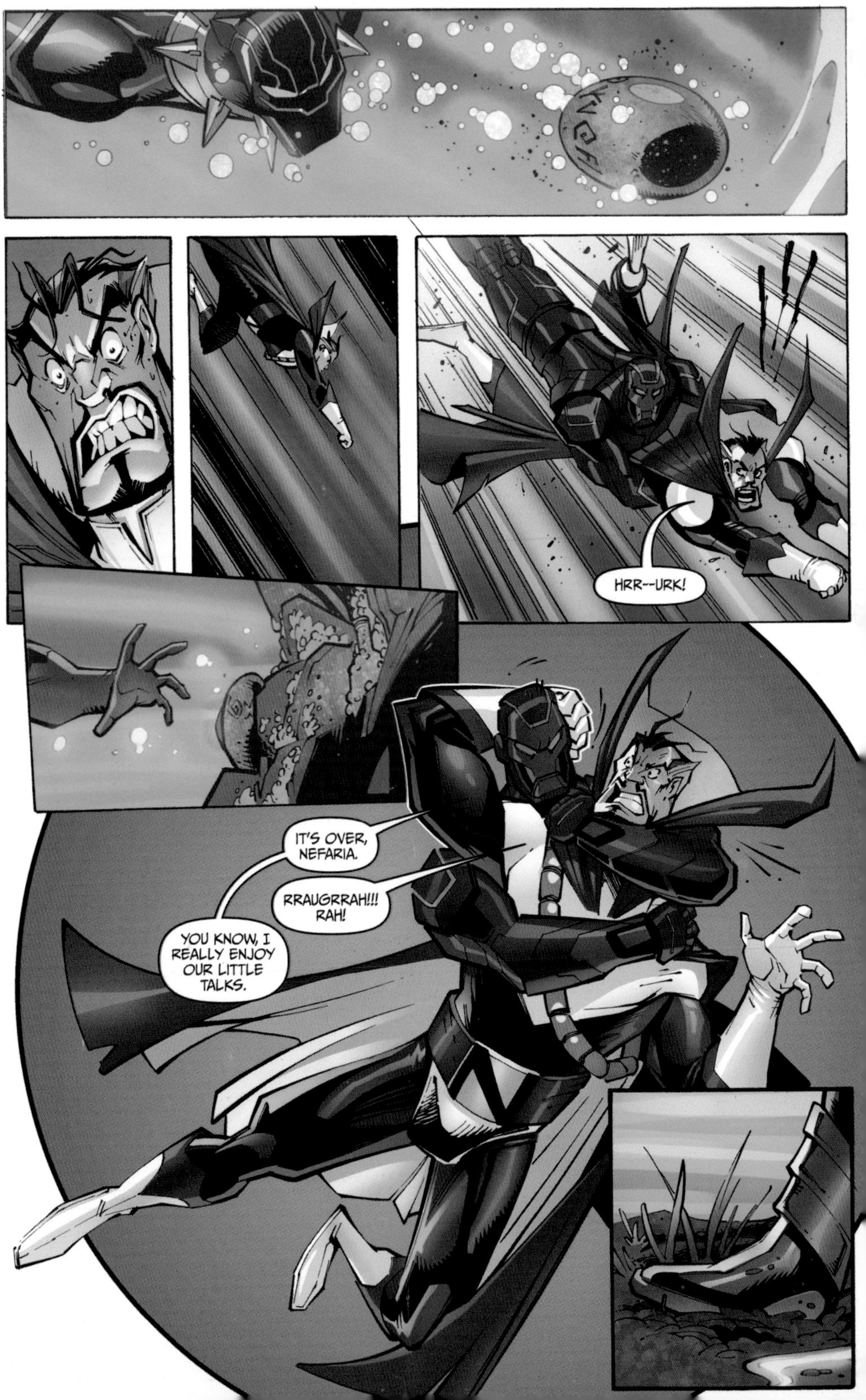
HRR--URK!
IT'S OVER, NEFARIA.
RRAUGRRAH!!! RAH!
YOU KNOW, I REALLY ENJOY OUR LITTLE TALKS.

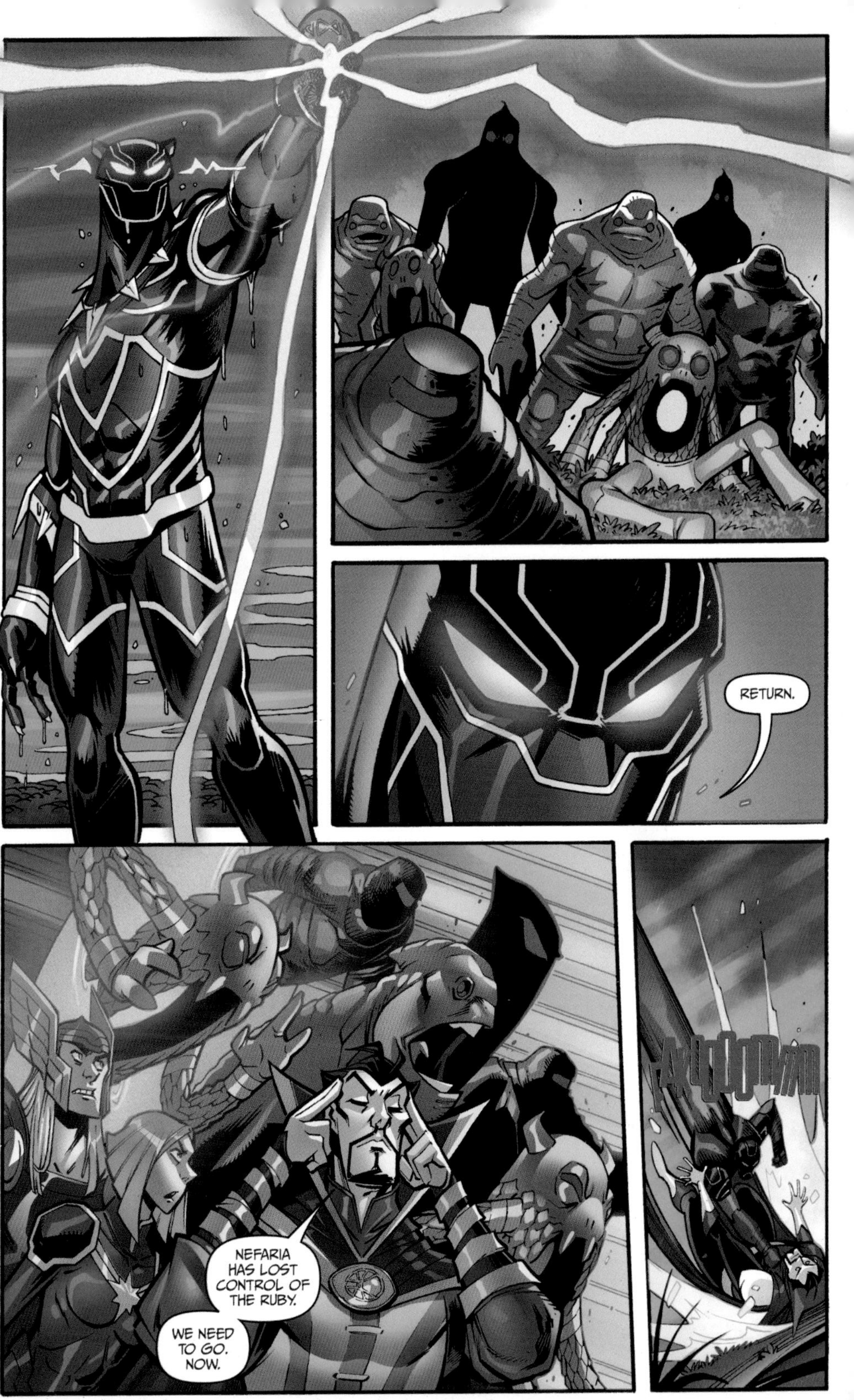
RETURN.
NEFARIA HAS LOST CONTROL OF THE RUBY.
WE NEED TO GO. NOW.

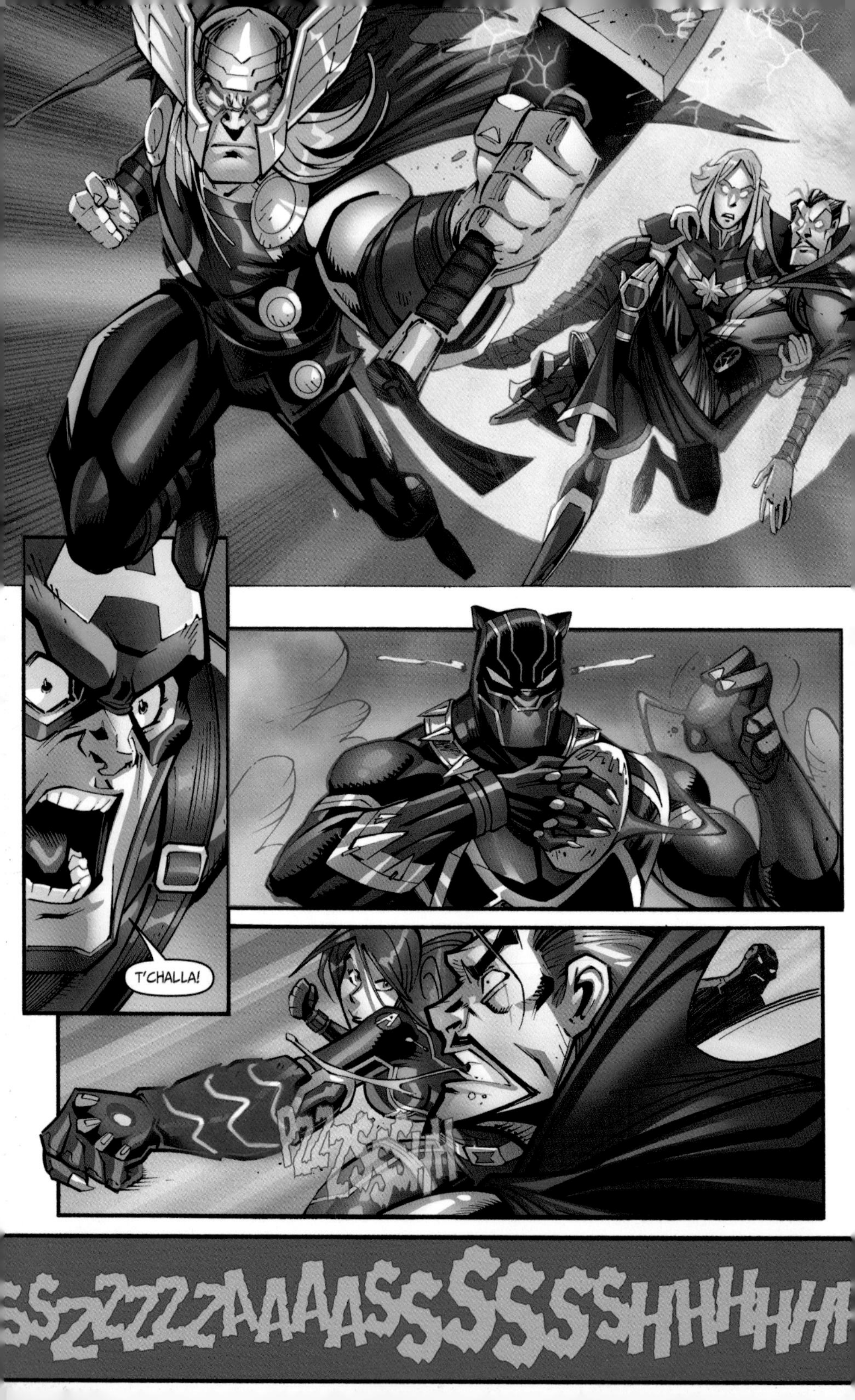
T'CHALLA!
SSZZZZZAAAASSSSSHHHHH

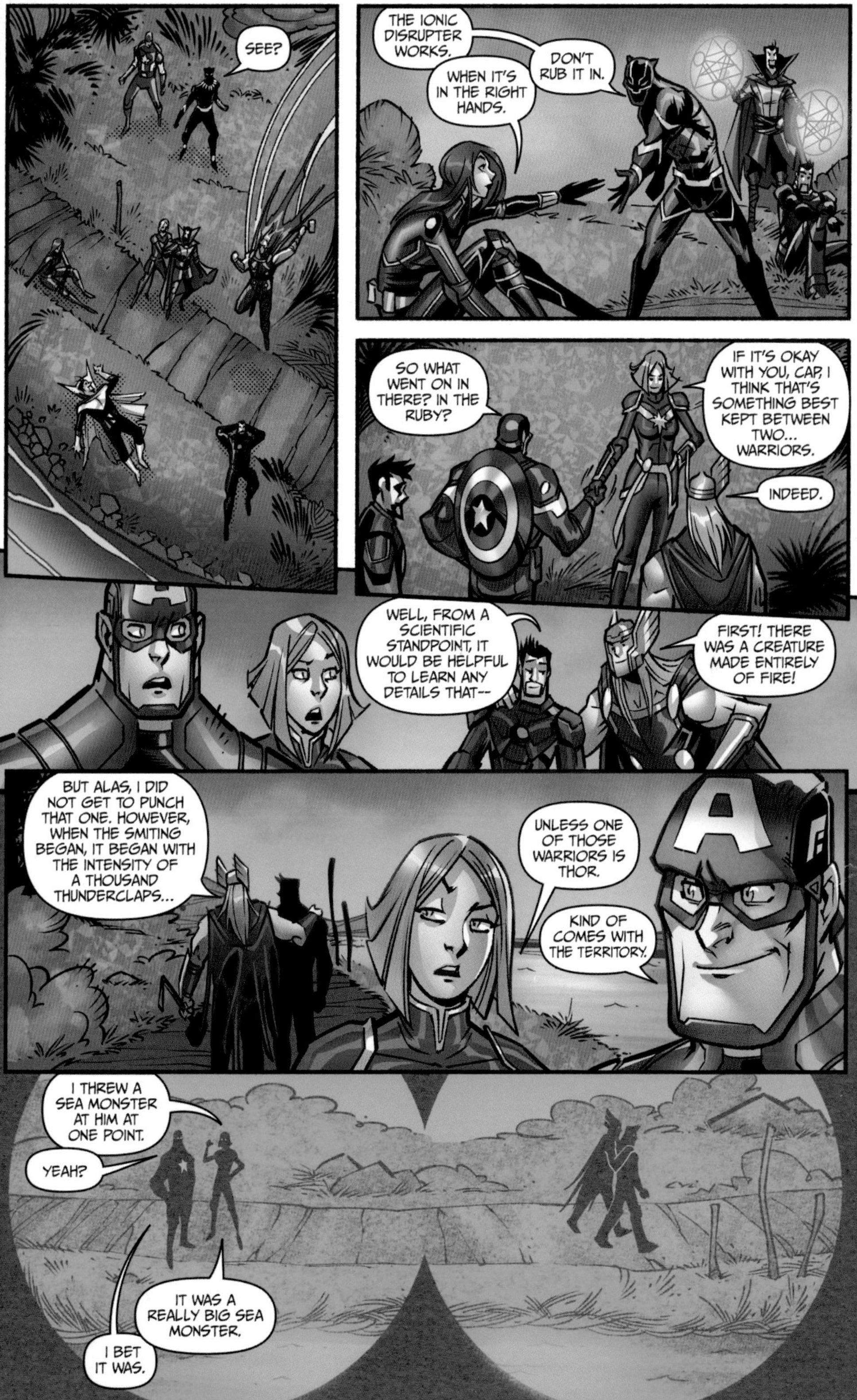

SEE?
THE IONIC DISRUPTER WORKS.
DON'T RUB IT IN.
WHEN IT'S IN THE RIGHT HANDS.
SO WHAT WENT ON IN THERE? IN THE RUBY?
IF IT'S OKAY WITH YOU, CAP, I THINK THAT'S SOMETHING BEST KEPT BETWEEN TWO... WARRIORS.
INDEED.
WELL, FROM A SCIENTIFIC STANDPOINT, IT WOULD BE HELPFUL TO LEARN ANY DETAILS THAT--
FIRST! THERE WAS A CREATURE MADE ENTIRELY OF FIRE!
BUT ALAS, I DID NOT GET TO PUNCH THAT ONE. HOWEVER, WHEN THE SMITING BEGAN, IT BEGAN WITH THE INTENSITY OF A THOUSAND THUNDERCLAPS...
UNLESS ONE OF THOSE WARRIORS IS THOR.
KIND OF COMES WITH THE TERRITORY.
I THREW A SEA MONSTER AT HIM AT ONE POINT.
YEAH?
IT WAS A REALLY BIG SEA MONSTER.
I BET IT WAS.

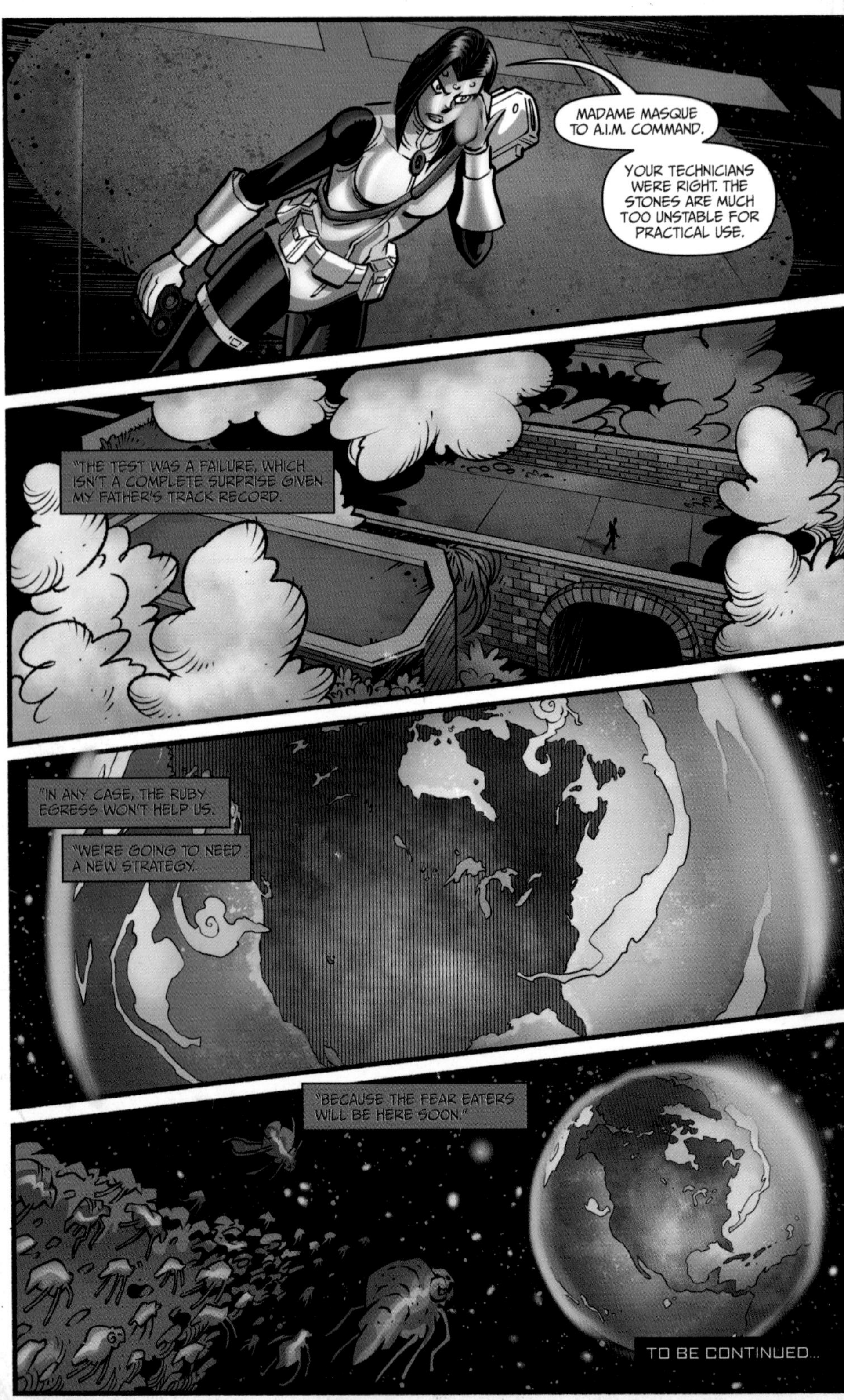
MADAME MASQUE TO A.I.M. COMMAND.
YOUR TECHNICIANS WERE RIGHT. THE STONES ARE MUCH TOO UNSTABLE FOR PRACTICAL USE.
"THE TEST WAS A FAILURE, WHICH ISN'T A COMPLETE SURPRISE GIVEN MY FATHER'S TRACK RECORD.
"IN ANY CASE, THE RUBY EGRESS WON'T HELP US.
"WE'RE GOING TO NEED A NEW STRATEGY.
"BECAUSE THE FEAR EATERS WILL BE HERE SOON."
TO BE CONTINUED...

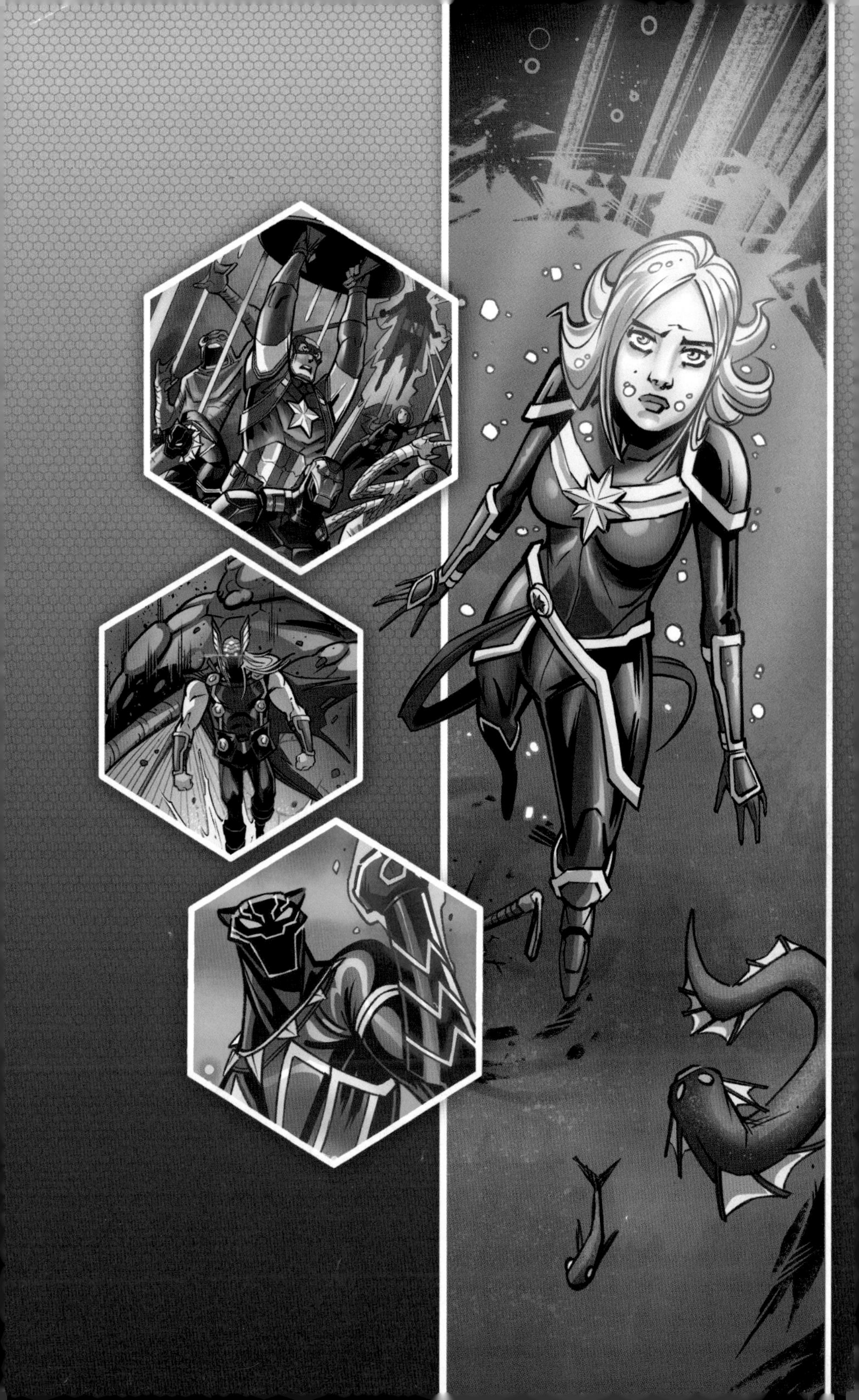

ART BY: CHAD THOMAS
COLORS BY: NICK FILARDI

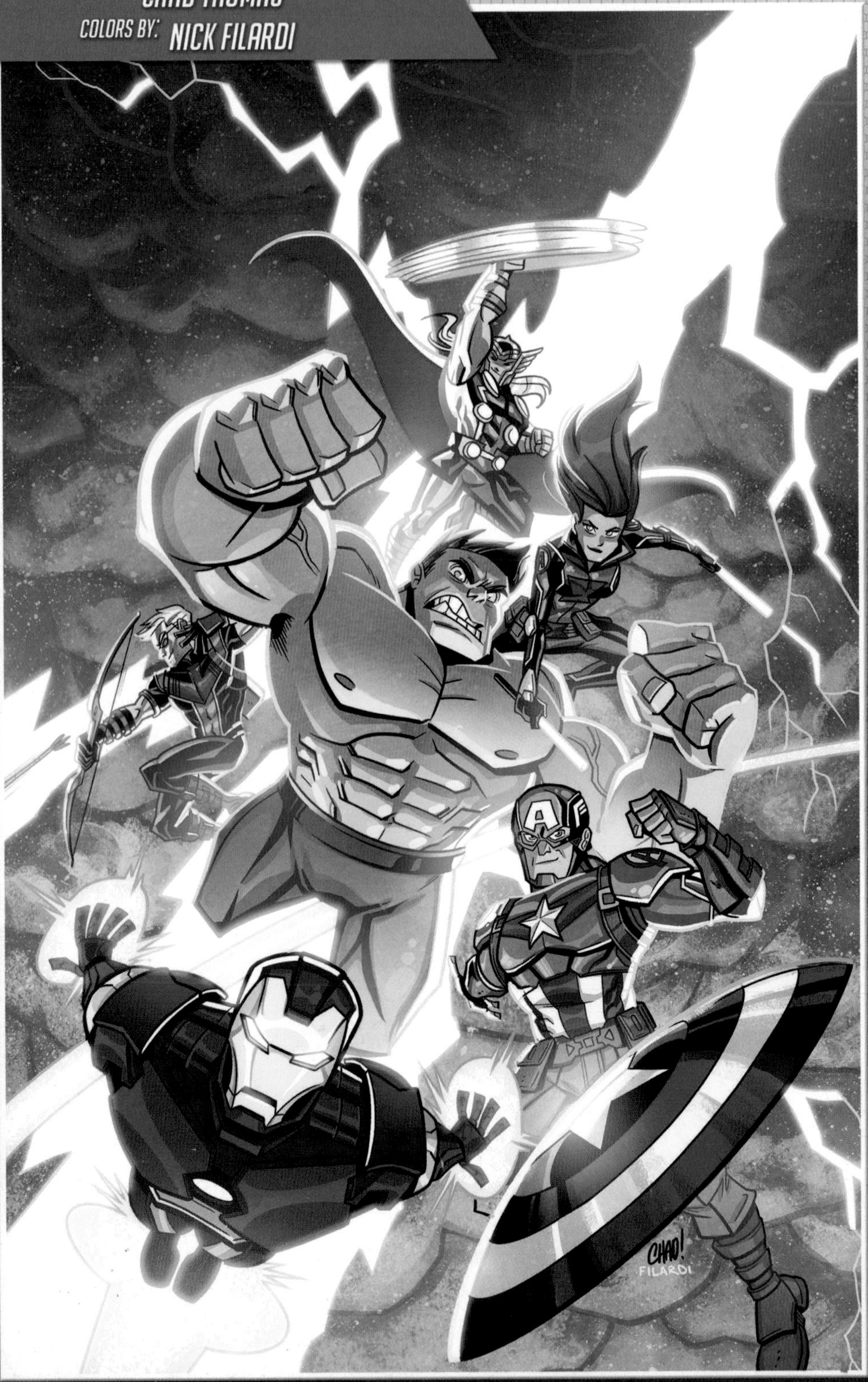
CHAD!
FILARDI

ART BY: BILLY MARTIN

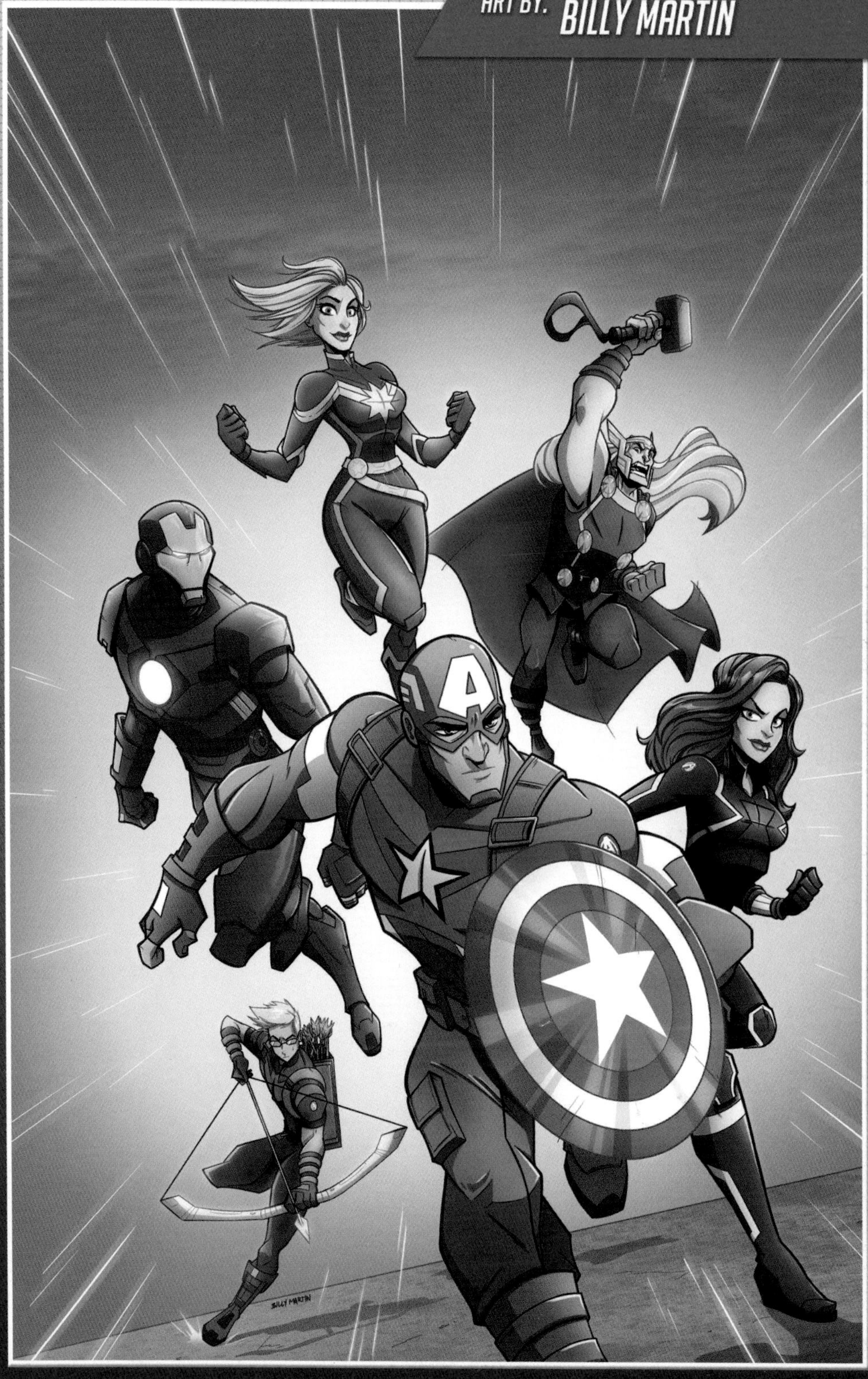
BILLY MARTIN

ART BY: TONY FLEECS

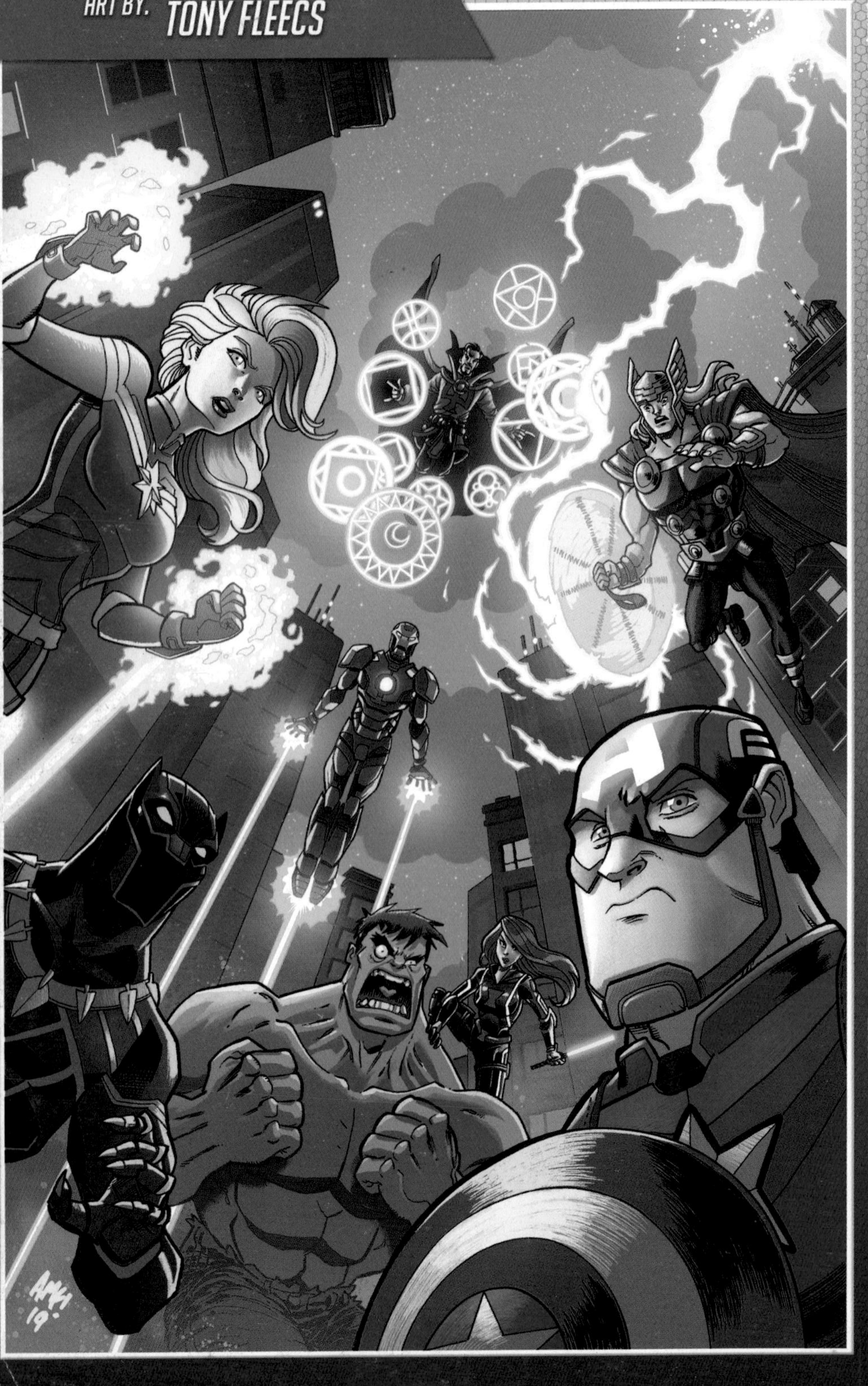